Bound by His Touch

Bound by His Touch

R. Michelle

www.urbanbooks.net

Urban Books, LLC
114 Norman Ave.
Amityville, NY 11701

ISBN 13: 978-1-64556-794-3
EBOOK ISBN: 978-1-64556-795-0

First Trade Paperback Printing April 2026
Printed in the United States of America

10 9 8 7 6 5 4 3 2 1

Distributed by Kensington Publishing Corp.
Submit Orders to:
Customer Service
400 Hahn Road
Westminster, MD 21157-4627
Phone: 1-800-733-3000
Fax: 1-800-659-2436

The authorized representative in the EU for product safety and compliance
Is eucomply OU, Parnu mnt 139b-14, Apt 123
Tallinn, Berlin 11317, hello@eucompliancepartner.com

Bound by His Touch

R. Michelle

Chapter 1

De'Maceo

"Bro, I swear to God, you can't pull that," my brother, Mario, said.

I looked at that nigga and laughed. I could get any female out here, and this nigga picks jailbait. I ain't gon' lie, li'l mama was thick in all the right places, and she had the cutest smile, but the fact remained: she was seventeen, and I was twenty-one. I liked my life too much to be in somebody's jail for fucking with that young-ass girl.

"I'm not about to mess with that young-ass girl. You trying to get a nigga locked under the jail. Come on, nah. I'm not about to fuck with her."

"Pussy," he mumbled.

"Far from a pussy, but I'm not fucking with that young-ass girl. End of discussion."

Mario kept talking shit until they crossed the street, and I got nervous as fuck. The other girl headed straight for Mario, while the girl he wanted me to holler at just stood there looking at the ground. I looked her over from head to toe. Li'l mama was thick as fuck in that short-ass dress she had on.

Ol' girl that was talking to my brother asked, "Mario, you rude as fuck. Who is this?" She was talking to him, but she was looking at me.

"My fault. Maceo, this my girl, Erian. Erian, this my big brother, Maceo."

"Hi, Maceo. This is my best friend, Saiyah." Erian elbowed her, and she looked up at me and waved.

"Um, Erian. I need to change these clothes before my daddy see them. I don't want to hear his mouth. I'm just going to go home."

I looked up the block and seen three niggas coming our way. I didn't have no heat on me, so I needed to get them outta here.

"Aye, Mario, it's getting late, bro. You need to shake this really quick," I said, nodding my head down the street. I guess they peeped, and Saiyah grabbed her friend. They started walking off for a safe distance.

"So, what's all this I hear about y'all working my block?"

I looked up in this clown Wu's face. "Yo' block? Fuck nigga, you ain't got no block. If it is yo' block, where you been at? I've been on this same post for the last twelve hours. Where the fuck have you been? Gone move around, bro." I waved my hand at that nigga. I wasn't about to beef with that nigga. He was a pussy, and he knew it.

"It doesn't matter where the fuck I was. Everybody know these my blocks."

"Who the fuck is everybody, nigga? Ain't nobody fucking out here, so I'm not about to sit up here and chit-chat with you, nigga. What's up?" I had already sold all the shit that I had, and so had my brother.

That nigga started taking his shirt off, and I looked at him. Yeah, he was a clown. He walked over to me and was all in my face. I looked at that nigga and smirked.

I heard some noise to my left, and that's when I saw Mario tussling with the other nigga. That bitch-ass nigga, Wu, took that as his chance to swing on me. I ducked and hit that nigga in his stomach, winding him. I heard screaming and turned around. The other nigga was behind me, about to sneak me with a knife. I punched that nigga in his face, and he fell to the ground, leaking. I saw a couple of more niggas coming up the block, and Mario had already knocked dude out.

Saiyah and Erian were running back to us.

"Get y'all stuff and come on, y'all can come to my house." Saiyah grabbed my hand, and we all took off toward her house.

After running about three blocks, I saw the niggas wasn't behind us, so we slowed down. She pulled us through an alley and up the gangway of her house. She told us to wait until she checked to see if her parents were home. We waited for about five minutes until she came out and told us to come in.

"My parents are going to be gone for the rest of the week. They're at a conference for preachers in Puerto Rico." She shrugged, and I nodded my head at her.

"Y'all can sit in the basement. It's down those stairs and to the left. Erian know the way."

Erian got up, and Mario followed her down the stairs. Saiyah was moving around the kitchen, and I watched her. Her hips were nice and wide, her long hair hung to the middle of her back, and her skin looked smooth. But them buns! Baby girl had some cheeks on her. Her booty jiggled in the pants every time she moved.

"Oh my God! You scared the fuck outta me. Why you ain't go downstairs? I was getting us some snacks."

"We need to get up outta here. Aye—"

"Why you in a rush to leave?"

"Baby girl, I'm twenty-one, you're seventeen. Ain't no way I'm supposed to be up in here with you. You jailbait."

"I guess you're right. Maybe you should leave. Erian, they have to go."

I looked at her sideways because I ain't understand where the attitude came from.

"Aye, Erian, hol' up! Let me talk to yo' girl real quick." Getting up, I walked over to her. Looking down at her short ass, I laughed. She was a whole foot shorter than me.

"What's up with the attitude, shorty?"

"I'm just saying. My age shouldn't have anything to do with how a person feel about me. You're twenty-one. Prolly barely twenty-one. I'll be eighteen soon, but that's beside the point. If I liked you, I would let you know. I'm not that much younger than you." She wasn't even looking me in my face. She was looking behind me.

Placing my hand under her chin, I pulled it up. "One, you looking behind me. I ain't back there. Two, I hear what you saying, but what you feel and the law are two different things. Besides, how you know I'm feeling you?"

"I don't, but I know I'm feeling you, though. This isn't my first time seeing you."

I thought about what she said. I didn't remember seeing her at all.

"It was you and a couple of other guys. Y'all was on the corner, and one dude tried talking to me, but you stopped him. It was about two weeks ago."

I knew what day she was talking about. I swore, if I ever caught shorty, it would be a smash-and-dash type of thing.

"Oh, shit. That was you? Li'l ma, you gotta add some more fabric to your shorts."

"Those are Erian's, and my clothes accidentally fell into bleach at her house, so I had to put them on."

"Oh, damn! Well, I'm glad you made it home safely then, but I ain't know you was that young. Mario can get away with it. He's twenty, so they ain't gon' come for him like they would me."

"Oh, ok. Well, y'all can leave if you want to."

I'm not gon' lie. I didn't want to leave her now because I wanted to see if I could slide in real quick. I ain't had no pussy in a minute. I knew shorty wasn't no virgin, and she was most likely down for anything. It was always the shy, reserved girls who were hoes or had more bodies on them than a li'l bit, and her daddy was a preacher. Yeah, she was giving it up.

"I mean, we can chill up here if you want to. Unless you want to chill in your bedroom," I told her, licking my lips. I promise y'all don't know how hard I was trying to control myself. I lowkey wanted to bend shorty over, hit that shit from the back.

"Um, we can chill in my room." She grabbed my hand and led me up the stairs. We walked down a hall before we got to a door, and we walked up another set of stairs. Her bedroom was in the attic, but it was big as fuck and clean.

"Take yo' shoes off."

I slipped my shoes off and looked around. She had a king-sized bed, so I sat down on it. She went to close the lower door before coming up and changing clothes in her bathroom. Then she got on the bed with me. Instead of lying next to me, she sat in my lap.

"What's up, shorty? Why you sitting on a nigga?"

"I don't know, but I feel safe around you for some odd reason. I'm comfortable and don't have to worry about the next nigga knowing our business, or my business for that matter. Plus, I think you're cute and been wanting to kiss you for the longest."

I ain't expect her to say all that. Leaning forward, I placed my lips to hers and let it linger for a while before I pulled her bottom lip in between mine and slowly sucked on it. I felt her adjust in my lap, and I knew she felt me brick up. A moan escaped through her lips, and

I said fuck it. Wrapping my arms around her waist, I slipped my tongue in between her lips and pulled her closer to me. Flipping us over, I aligned our bodies and pulled from the kiss.

Reaching my hand underneath her dress, I pulled her panties to the side and played with her pearl. I looked down at her. Her cheeks were bright red, and she was holding her breath.

"Breathe, ma. You good," I stated. Moving a li'l lower, I slipped a finger inside her as I kissed all over her neck.

"Wait, Mace. I ain't never did this before."

Stopping, I looked at her. One, she called me Mace. Two, I know she wasn't telling me she was virgin.

"Yo' ass a virgin? How?" I snapped, pulling my finger out of her.

"What do you mean, how? Did you think because I was seventeen that I was busting it open for every nigga out here? I ain't them bitches you be running through. The fuck!" she snapped as she pushed me away and got up off the bed, storming in the bathroom.

Looking at the nightstand, I saw the tissue and wiped my finger off before going to the bathroom and knocking on the door.

"Saiyah! Come out the bathroom, man."

"Why? You can leave now," she snapped.

This was why I didn't want to deal with no young-ass girl.

"Get yo' ass out the bathroom, man. I'm trying to talk to you."

I heard the knob turn, then I stood back, and she stormed past me.

"What you want?"

"First off, lower your mothafucking tone. And I'm trying to see what's up. Why you really bring a nigga up here?"

"I ain't wanna be a virgin no more, and I refuse to lose it to one of them lame-ass niggas at school. Besides, Erian always talks about what Mario can do and how great he is, so I figured you'd be just as good."

I chuckled because here I was trying to use her for some pussy, and she was trying to use me, too. If her pussy was pure, then that shit was going to be wet and tight, and it had been a minute since I slid up in some virgin pussy. I might just have to break her in.

"Mannn! Are yo' parents really gone for the rest of the week? I saw pictures as we were coming up the stairs that you got two younger siblings. Where they at?"

"They're probably with them. They always leave me here alone."

"A'ight, I'll make you a deal. Let's get to know each other first because I don't want you to regret this shit. I want you to get to know me so you will feel more comfortable with just having sex with me."

She nodded her head. "Well, they won't be back anytime soon being that they just left this morning. But I do have one request."

"What's up? I asked as I sat on the bed.

"I want you to teach me everything without missing anything. I want to make the most of this experience. You're a little older and patient, so I want the whole sexual experience."

My dick bricked up. "It's going to take more than one night to teach you all of that."

"Well, we better to get to knowing each other then," she said, sitting on the bed next to me and handing me the remote.

Chapter 2

De'Marrion

"Fuck!" I yelled out as Erian slid up and down my pole.

"Nah, you talked all that shit, Mario," Erian said to me as she rode my dick in a split.

I wasn't even paying her ass no mind. I was concentrating on not cumming. She had caught me in a weak moment, and I forgot to put a condom on.

"Erian, slow down," I gritted out, but she wasn't paying me no mind. Placing my hands under her legs, I bounced Erian up and down.

Her head fell back in pure ecstasy. "Mario! I'm about to cum," she yelled out.

"Fuck! Me, too!" I growled out as she came all over my dick. Seeing her cum leak down my pole caused him to release my own, right into her.

"Fuck, man! I knew I should've stopped yo' ass."

"Shut up! I'm on the pill anyway."

I mugged the fuck outta her. "Then why the fuck am I using condoms then?"

She looked at me like I was crazy. "Because, nigga, I'm not trying to be that one percent that comes up pregnant. Today was a one-time thing."

"The fuck if it is. I'm going raw dog in my pussy every chance I get."

She rolled her eyes, but I didn't give a fuck. My pussy, my rules.

"But what yo' girl on with my brother, though? You know he see her ass as jailbait."

"I don't know, but when I went up there to check, she had locked and closed her room door, so who knows what they are into. Yah, a virgin, though."

"What the fuck? My brother doesn't need those kinds of problems."

"Chill out, bae. I'm sure she told him. Saiyah ain't all as shy as she makes herself out to be. Trust and believe that. If she wants Maceo, she's going to tell him what's up."

"A'ight. If yo' girl get on some fatal attraction shit, I ain't got no problem with killing her over my brother."

She giggled and went into the bathroom.

De'Maceo, or Maceo as I call him, is my big brother. Same mother, same father. He was all I had in this fucked up world, and I refused to let anything happen to him. My mother was a fucking coke head, and I didn't even know my pops. The only reason that I knew my brother and I had the same pops was because my mama used to tell us that shit. We hustled to get the shit we need, everything my brother and I had. We both had other jobs besides selling drugs. My brother worked as a janitor, cleaning schools at night, while I worked at Wendy's, and that's where I sold most of my drugs, through the drive-through. I hadn't been caught so far, and I didn't plan to. I wasn't trying to sit in nobody's fucking cell. It just wasn't in me to do it.

"Here," Erian said, handing me a towel to wipe myself off.

"What you trying to do today? You know I gotta go to work later?" I asked Erian.

"We can go grab your uniform, and you can leave from my house since your job is closer to my house."

"Yeah, we can do that. Let me let my brother know that we gone."

Grabbing my iPhone off the table, I sent my brother a message.

Maceo: Aight, bro. I'll get up with you later. I gotta tell you about this wild ass shit.

Me: You are talking about shorty. You know her ass a virgin.

Maceo: Yeah, I know nigga. That's why I told you I gotta tell you about this wild ass shit.

Me: Aight, then. I work from 9:30-3:30.

Maceo: I'll be looking out for you. If not, hit my line before you leave so I can have you slide back through here. You know it's spring break for them.

Me: Word? You spending the night? But nah, I ain't know that. I'll hit you later.

Putting my phone in my pocket, I saw Erian looking at me.

"When you were gon' tell me that yo' ass had spring break?"

"I did tell you. You were too busy trying to get some pussy." She giggled.

"Man, a'ight. Bring yo' nappy-headed ass on. We gotta slide by my crib and get my shit, and we can head to yours. Is yo' mama home?"

"Nah, she's on a vacation with her husband."

"Oh, shit. You mean a nigga can spend the night?" I inquired.

"Yeah, so grab all you need."

I nodded my head, grabbed her hand, and we headed up the stairs and out of the house.

Chapter 3

Saiyah

A Few Days Later . . .

I couldn't believe that I had convinced him to go through with it. I had seen Maceo around more than he thought. Everything about him screamed sexy D-boy, and I just wanted to see what some of them older girls who stood at the bus stop be talking about. I knew I was tired of being a virgin, and there was no way in hell that I was going to allow one of them lame-ass boys from school to do it. They didn't know a pussy hole from an asshole, and I wouldn't even dare let them near me.

Moving around my room, I got everything ready before lying in bed.

"Yo, Yah. What you doing, ma? Why you leave the front door unlock . . ." he trailed off when he saw me lying across the bed in nothing but my panties. He licked his lips, and I smiled on the inside because that meant he was interested.

"You sure you ready for this?"

I nodded my head.

"What you wanna learn first?" he asked, removing his chain from around his neck, pulling his shirt over his head, and pulling his pants off.

"Well, Erian said all dudes liked head, so I guess we can start there."

"One, that's true. But two, you don't give every nigga head. Three, are you sure?"

"Yeah. Stop asking that, Mace."

He sat on the bed and pulled me to the ground in front of him. "Pull him out then, and make sure your mouth is wet. And cover your teeth. No nigga likes when all he feels is teeth scrape up and down his dick."

Nodding my head, I pulled him out. I knew Maceo was huge, but not this huge. I looked up at him skeptically, and he laughed.

"It's alright, Yah. You ain't supposed to fit all me in your mouth, just the majority. Now, come on, man."

Closing my eyes, I slowly took him into my mouth, remembering everything that he said. I heard a hissing noise like he was in pain. Opening my eyes, I looked at him, but his head was thrown back.

He looked down at me. "Why you stop?" he asked.

"I thought I was hurting you."

"Hell nah! Keep going! Relax your jaws more."

Closing my eyes, I went back to giving him head. I had recently watched porn, maybe a time or two, and I wanted to see if I could fit him further into my mouth. Surprisingly, I didn't gag, so I kept going, and I heard him start cussing. Relaxing my throat and jaws a little bit, I thought about the porn videos and what I read online, and I did what they said. Taking him out and putting him back in, I made sure my mouth was wet as I proceeded to suck him up.

"Fuck! Yah, hold up. Saiyah! Stop!"

Sucking in my jaws, I opened my eyes and looked up at him as I continued.

"Oh my God! Fuck! Saiyah, stop!" he yelled out as he pushed my head away from his dick.

"What? Did I do something wrong?" I asked him.

"Hell yeah. This ain't yo' first time sucking dick. Where the fuck you learn that shit at? And you don't get no gag reflexes. What the fuck?" he snapped.

"What are you talking about?"

"Yo' ass giving me head like a pro at sucking dick. How the fuck did you learn to do it that fast?"

"I watched a tutorial on giving head on a porn site."

"How many did you watch?"

"About six, but it was this good one, and it taught me the other stuff I just did."

"Yeah, well, I was about to cum in yo' mouth if I hadn't pushed yo' head away. Don't let no nigga do that shit if you don't want to. But um, get on the bed. Since you a virgin, I'm almost certain you ain't never had yo' pussy ate."

I shook my head.

"Well, come on then. I'll make an exception for you."

He helped me up on the bed before removing his boxers and grabbing a condom out of his wallet. When he pulled me to the edge of the bed, I closed my eyes. I felt his tongue touch my clit. I didn't know what he was doing, but it felt good. Grabbing the back of his head, I pulled him closer. The feeling below and in the pit of my stomach was something I had never felt before.

"Oh my God! Mace, right there," I cried out, as he licked in this one particular spot.

Opening my eyes, I watched him and felt him dip his tongue in and out of my hole before placing kisses all over my clit. The feeling was getting stronger, and I couldn't take it.

"Mace, stop!" I tried pushing his head away, but instead, he locked his hands across my stomach and kept going.

"Mace! Oh, my God, Mace!" I yelled out as my entire body shook.

Mace let me go and stood back with a smirk on his face. "That's one," he said before he rolled the condom on, moving back onto the bed.

He climbed on top of me. Turning my face towards his, I pulled him closer to me, then kissed him.

"You got two options, Yah. You can get on top and control the movement, or you can let me put it really quick and go from there."

"Put it in real quick. I want you to teach me how to ride after the pain goes away."

"Count to five for me," he said, placing himself at my entrance.

"One . . . two . . ." Right as I was counting to three, I felt him push all the way in. He stilled once he got inside. I felt the tears escaping my eyes, but he wiped 'em away with his kisses.

"You said you wanted to learn everything, so this first time, I'ma make love to you." Leaning down, he placed a kiss on my lips and proceeded to make love to me.

He took his time exploring every inch of my body. The feeling of him was something I would cherish for the rest of my life. It was too early, way too early to be in love, but I was enjoying every moment that he was giving me.

I collapsed on the bed, my entire body tired. Ever since Maceo came over, we had been going at it. I was sore as hell down there, and Maceo had long ago run out of condoms. I knew I should've stopped him, but he said he would go and get me a morning after pill. I didn't know much about it, nor about Maceo, but I trusted him, if that made sense.

"Aye, Yah! You need to get in the shower. I know you're sore as hell down there," he told me, rolling over, and I looked at him and smiled.

"What yo' ass smiling for?"

"I wanted to thank you. You didn't have to do this, Mace, but you did, and I appreciate you for giving me the time of my life and showing me what it means to be made love to and fucked. Now I'll know when I meet the next man."

Maceo nodded his head and didn't say anything. He got up, went into the bathroom, and turned on the water. A couple of minutes later, he came back, picked me up, and placed me in the tub, then left the bathroom. I wondered if I had said something wrong to him.

Relaxing in the tub a little bit, I washed my body before standing up and taking a shower. Grabbing my towel off the rack, I got out, and Maceo was standing at the door. I slipped on the floor and almost fell, but Mace helped me.

"What the hell, De'Maceo? Why you are standing at the door like a creep?"

"Man, I shouldn't have done that shit for you, but here goes yo' pill. Take it so I can dip."

"Um, okay. Did you bring me something to drink?"

He handed me a Calypso strawberry lemonade and went back into my room. I took the pill and finished drying off.

When I walked into my room, Maceo was sitting on my bed. "Well, if you're ready to leave, you can leave, Mace."

"What you trying to get rid of me for?" He spazzed.

I just stared at him. "That's why I'm getting rid of you, Maceo. What do you have an attitude for? I thought you understood. Besides, I used you as much as you used me. I wanted to lose my virginity, and you wanted some fresh, pure pussy. Ain't that what you said?"

"Man, I ain't never said that shit out loud to nobody but my fucking brother, and why you going through my shit anyways?"

"First, I ain't have to go through your shit. You left it open on your phone when yo' stupid ass dozed off, so don't ever come at me about going through your shit. I'm not your bitch, remember. No reason for me to be pressed over some dick."

"Man, fuck you, Yah, straight the fuck up."

"You seem mad. Why? Because you taught me all your li'l tricks and I'm about to have another nigga on lock when I find him?"

"You a straight-up hoe," he sniped.

"But you want me to be yo' hoe, though. Say it, Maceo. Say you want me to be yours, and I'll be yours. You're upset because you just wanted me for your own purposes, but I flipped it around on you."

"What the fuck ever. I gotta handle some business. I'll see you when I see you," he said, grabbing his jacket.

"Why are you scared, De'Maceo?"

"Because every woman I've encountered has broken my heart, and I'll be damned if a little girl breaks it, too," he snapped before walking off, leaving my heart in pieces.

Chapter 4

Erian

Saiyah had been moping around for some time now, and I couldn't believe it. Her and Maceo didn't even know each other that well, but they were both around here looking like some sad-ass puppies.

If those days that they spent together impacted them this hard, then I knew it was real. It had been a month since whatever happened. They were refusing to talk about it, but I had a feeling that it was deeper than what Mario and I even touched on. The sadness in Saiyah's eyes hurt me because, as a best friend, I was supposed to make it better. Yet, I didn't know what was going on or what happened.

So, I was going to ask this last time and see if she told me. "Saiyah, why are you walking around here mad at the world?"

"I'm not mad. I'm just bothered."

"You upset about Maceo? Want me to cuss him out for you?"

"It's not all about Maceo. It's how I feel now that he isn't in my life. What I had with him was real, even if it seemed like a fairytale to everyone else. What I felt for him, I may never feel again."

"What happened between y'all? He's walking around the same way, like he lost his best friend. Was it that intense?"

"Yeah, it was. And I don't want to talk about what happened," she said, blowing the subject off.

I decided to leave it alone. "Well, we are going out tonight to dinner and a movie. You coming?"

"Is this like a date type of thing?"

"No, we all are just going."

"Who is we?"

"Mario, Briana, Amarion, and that's it."

"Sounds like some date stuff. I'ma just stay at home."

"Alright, Saiyah, have it your way." I continued eating my food until lunch was over, and then we headed to our lockers.

I saw our friend, Briana, was already at our lockers.

"Hey, bitches! So, are we all on for the movie and dinner tonight?"

"I'm in, but Saiyah isn't going, so it'll just be us."

"Saiyah, what's the issue?" Briana asked her

"I'm going to be a third wheel. It'll be you and Amarion, a couple, then Mario and Erian. Need I say more? I'ma just go home early. I'll see y'all later." Saiyah closed her locker and walked off.

"Wow! What is wrong with her?" Briana asked.

"I have no clue, but I'm going to find out."

Slamming my locker, I rushed off to class. I sent Maceo a message to meet me after school. I was going to get to the bottom of it. Saiyah's parents weren't at home for the next two weeks. Hell, her parents were never at home, so her and Maceo were about to fix this problem. I couldn't deal with these sorry-ass looks on their faces.

I endured my last class, but my mind kept drifting to Saiyah. I didn't understand how she was this upset over their "situationship" when she didn't even know much about him. I was just confused. I'd been messing around with Mario for a while, and I knew Maceo, but not well enough. The day I pretended not to know him was simply because Saiyah was trying to avoid crossing the street, but when I saw my man, all bets were off at that point. I had to fake introduce them, but I saw the look in his eyes and Saiyah's. They wanted each other.

As soon as the bell rang for the end of the day, I grabbed my backpack and rushed out of the class. I was excited to be leaving for the weekend.

Walking outside, I saw Maceo leaning against his car while bitches tried to get his attention. When I saw the biggest hoe, Yetti, trying to get his attention, I moved quicker to get to him. She was smiling all up in his face. I muffed her to the side. I wanted the bitch to get tough so I could have a reason to beat her ass. She looked at me and rolled her eyes. Maceo shook his head and got in the car.

"I would advise you to steer clear of that one. He's taken," I said to Yetti since she was standing there.

"I don't even want shit from Maceo. I was just trying to cop until your thirsty ass came up."

I laughed at her ass because she knew damn well I was with Mario. "Cute, boo! Real cute. Next time, I'ma beat yo' ass. Tread lightly, hoe," I said to her before I pulled the car door open and got inside.

"Why I have to meet you? I hope you ain't on no other shit because I'll tell my brother quick as hell," Maceo said when I slid into the seat of his new car.

I looked at him and rolled my eyes. "Boy, I don't want yo' ass, but I need you to check on Saiyah for me. She hasn't come to school in a couple of days, and I don't know what's wrong. I can't go over there because Mario is picking me up in about fifteen minutes. Can you please do it?" I lied to him and begged at the same time.

"No, I got some shit to handle. Why one of y'all other friends can't do it?"

"Maceo, stop! Whatever you and Saiyah had must've impacted y'all both greatly. That girl is literally a zombie around here. Can you please go and talk to her? I don't know what happened because she won't tell me. Can you fix it, please?" I begged him.

"Aight, man. Aight. How she gon' know I'm coming? What about her people?"

"They gone. And no, no one is home. Just pop up, Mace. Let me know if she's alright. Your brother is about to be pulling up any minute now, so I gotta go. But Maceo, I'm letting you know, if you hurt my best friend any more than you have now, you'll regret it." And with that, I got out of the car, and he pulled off. I prayed that he would go to check on Saiyah.

Later that night, we pulled up to the restaurant. I saw Briana and Amarion waiting outside for us. Mario parked and helped me out of the car. We walked over, they dapped each other up, and we headed inside. Since we had reservations, we got seated immediately.

I was getting ready to pick up the menu when I heard some bitch say, "So that's why Mario ain't answering my call? He got him a young bitch."

Turning to my right, I saw a group of bitches staring at us. I was about to say something, but one of them bitches got bold and approached the table.

"Hey, Mario! Hey, Amarion. What's up with y'all?"

"What's up is his dick that I ride every night. If you don't need nothing else, dismiss my nigga name from your vocabulary. Next time it leaves your lips, you just might end up on the Channel 7 news," Briana said to ol' girl. I laughed because that bitch's face dropped.

“Hold up, bitc—”

“What do you want, Pate?” Mario asked her.

“I’m trying to figure out why you stopped fucking with me, and then you are messing with this little-ass girl.” She pointed toward me.

I was about to get up, but Mario shook his head.

“Aight. I’ma tell you three reasons why. One, I like my pussy tight and fitting around my dick. Yours can’t do that. Two, you burn niggas, and I love my dick too much to be burning. Three, you weren’t my bitch. You were something to do when there was nothing to do. Now, if you don’t mind, I want to finish eating with my woman and friends.”

“Really, Mario? You were just in this pussy last week. Matter of fact, your girl was blowing you up, and you were standing knee deep in this loose pussy.”

I looked at Mario to see his reaction, and he laughed. That pissed me off.

“Bitch, when? I haven’t fucked you since I started messing around with my girl. Why would I? Besides, I wasn’t even here last week. I got a week’s worth of receipts to prove that, on top of the bracelet on her wrist and earrings in her ears. Fuck would I lie to my woman for? And I’m not no cheating-ass nigga. When I got my woman, only pussy I need to climb in is hers, so get the fuck from our table before you end up floating in Lake Michigan. I put that on my soul, you lying, hoe-ass bitch.”

She looked at him, and the tears started to fall. Her friend must’ve seen what happened and came over and got her. “That’s fucked up, Mario,” the friend said.

“Nah, what’s mothafuckin’ sad is you still trying to be her best friend, knowing you swallowed my kids on multiple occasions. Fuck from over here. Y’all know I don’t make no threats. All promises. Now, move the fuck around, both of you hoes.”

They both walked away from the table.

“Order yo’ food, Erian. I don’t want to hear shit about no hoe that I ain’t fucking, nor do I love.”

“What you mean? That bitch came over here. I heard her before she came.”

“I’m not about to argue about no bitch that I’m not fucking. End of discussion. Order your food, and we can talk later.”

“Alright, Mario,” I snapped at him as I looked through the menu. Being petty as fuck, I ordered the most expensive thing on the menu.

Mario had me fucked up with all these extra bitches always coming out of the woodwork. If I found out that Mario was fucking around on me, I was breaking up with his ass. I didn’t want that type of drama in my life. I just prayed that it wasn’t the case.

Chapter 5

Maceo

I knew I shouldn't have fucking replied to Erian's ass. I was in the middle of getting me some head. When she sent that message, my shit deflated. I thought something was wrong, but it was only Saiyah. Now she had me going to check on Saiyah.

I knew I messed up with Saiyah when I walked out that day. My heart felt that pain, even though I didn't want to. Saiyah was cracking that ice around my heart, and if I could go back to that day, I would've walked back up those stairs when I started to. I'd been filtering through bitches like the names in a phone book, and none of them had held my attention. Every time I was about to fuck or get some head, I had to picture Saiyah or my dick would get soft. Every time I thought about the way her throat felt around the tip of my dick, I bricked up. She was beasting in the head department, and she learned all that shit from porn. And her li'l ass didn't have no gag reflexes. How she ain't know that shit, I would never know.

Saiyah lasted longer than any virgin I knew. That day, I fucked her eight hours straight, and that was thanks to good stamina and recovery time. I could still have energy afterward. After I entered her, I knew I had to leave a print on her soul. I made love to her for hours before I switched and fucked the shit outta her. During the whole lovemaking process, I caressed her soul, touched her heart, and made my name escape her lips.

I fucked up when I looked in her eyes. She had me stuck in a trance as I moved in and out of her. I regretted it because it wasn't my intention to fall for her. Everybody can say it was pussy, but if that was the case, why did I still feel that way?

Pulling up to her house, I sat in the car for a minute before turning the car off and jogging up the stairs. Ringing the doorbell, I waited for her to open the door. A few seconds later, I saw the blinds in the front window move, heard the locks being removed, and saw the door opening.

"Hi! How may I help you?" Saiyah asked, all formal.

"Uh, your girl was worried about you and asked me to come check on you."

"Well, I'm doing fine. Is there anything else you need?" she asked me nonchalantly.

I didn't know why, but it rubbed me the wrong way.

"I miss you, Yah, I do. And I'm sorry for how I've been doing you," I said sincerely.

"No, you don't, Maceo. But if you don't mind, I have some business to tend to." She looked behind her, and I got mad as fuck.

"What the fuck you looking back there for? Who back there, Saiyah?" I asked her.

"One, nobody is in here. Two, why are you here? Leave. Go be with the bitches you been with for the last month or so. You don't miss me." She looked behind her again.

Her stupid ass must've forgotten that I knew the lock was broken on the door. I pulled open the door and walked in, closing the door behind me. Stepping in front of her, I looked down.

"You don't miss me, Yah? All I can think about is you. I fucked up that night. You forgive me?"

"Mace, what do you want?"

I knew what she was asking without asking.

"Fuck it. I want you. I fucking want you, Yah," I said, pulling her to me and lowering my lips to hers. Walking us back toward the stairs, I led us up to her room and locked the door.

Stripping each other out of our clothes, we stood in the middle of her room, naked. Leaning up, she placed a kiss on my chest, up around my neck, before her lips landed on mine. I picked her up, and she wrapped her legs around my waist.

"Make love to me, Maceo."

"Say less."

Placing her down on the bed, I dropped to my knees and pushed her legs back until her knees touched her shoulders. Looking at her pussy lips marinating in her juices, I used my tongue to separate them. Running my tongue up and down her slit, I snaked my way back up to her clit before placing kisses on it.

"Mmmmaceooo!" she cried out as I slipped two fingers in her opening.

"This my pussy, Saiyah?"

I could hear her nodding her head. Wrapping my lips around her clit, I sucked it in, making her body rise off the bed.

"I'ma ask again. Is this pussy mine?"

"Yes! Yes! Oh my God! I gotta pee, Mace." She tried to shake outta my hold, but I pressed her legs further down. Her body was shaking, and just like that, she squirted. Still making the come-hither motion, she kept squirting until she was done.

Not giving her time to recover, I slid right into her tight and wet honey pot. Her walls slowly took me in as I pushed all the way to the hilt. Looking down at her, I moved slowly in and out of her.

"I'm sorry, ma. I fucked up," I spoke into her ear.

I felt her body shaking beneath me, but I knew it wasn't another orgasm. Looking down at her face, I saw she was crying. I felt like shit, but I kept making love to her.

"I promise I'ma make it up to you. I swear to God, I am. Stop crying, man," I said, kissing her tears away.

I kept looking at her age, and that had bypassed all the things I felt for her. Deep down, Saiyah made me feel shit that no other bitch had ever made me feel, and that was why I had to walk away. I couldn't allow a young girl to break my heart, but I knew Saiyah could, and she eventually would. For now, I would take that risk with heart.

"Oh my God! Maceo, I'm cumming!" Saiyah yelled out.

"Cum for me then," I said against her lips as I moved in and out of her rapidly. I felt my own nut rising. Saiyah was going to make me body any nigga who touched her, talked to her, even looked at her. That's the type of hold she had on me and my dick.

"Grrrr! Fuck, man!" I yelled out.

"I love you!" she yelled out as I came inside of her.

"What did you just say?" I asked her.

She looked at the wall, avoiding eye contact.

Pulling out of her, I went into the bathroom and wiped off. She came into the bathroom and started the shower.

"You need to pee, Saiyah."

She looked at me and sat on the toilet. After a few minutes, I could hear my nut sliding out of her into the toilet. Turning my back, I listened to her wipe before getting in the shower. Turning toward the shower, I watched her stand underneath the water. Contemplating what I wanted to do, I walked over to the shower door and pulled it open. Getting inside, I wanted to get back out that mufucka. That water was damn near scalding. I didn't know why women liked the water hot as fuck, but all I knew was it was burning the fuck outta me. Reaching for the knob, I turned it down.

"You mad at me, Yah?" I asked her.

"No," she said quietly.

"Don't get shy on me now. Tell me what's wrong."

"Nothing, De'Maceo."

I laughed at her attitude. "Oh, so when I'm fucking you, I'm Maceo or Mace, but since you got an attitude, I'm De'Maceo. I can't read minds, bae, so tell me what's up," I told her.

"I didn't mean for it to slip out that I loved you, but when I did, your entire body went rigid. You got stiff as wood. You didn't have to say it back. I don't even know if it's how I feel, but I'm going to assume that nobody has ever told you that they loved you."

I listened to her as she talked to me, then said, "I don't know what love is, like with a woman. Only person I ever loved was my brother, and I'm sure if he wasn't my brother, I wouldn't love him. So, nah, I ain't never been told I love you. You're the first one to say it."

"The first? Mace, you ain't ever been in love before?"

"The first one to break my heart was my mama, and my heart been cold ever since. I had this one girl, she swore she loved me, but that bitch was setting me up for her nigga. I dubbed that hoe and heard she ended up going to jail for a murder her nigga committed. His bitch ass had a whole wife and kids. He didn't want shit from her. So, nah, I ain't never met a woman who made me feel any type of way, until I met you."

"What you mean?"

"Yah, I can't say I love you, but I know I want you. Just give me some time."

She nodded her head and continued to take a shower. After a few minutes of being in the shower, having washed my body and rinsed off, I got out of the shower and grabbed a towel from her rack, then handed one to her.

Walking into her room, I dried off and put my clothes back on and sat on the bed. She came out a couple minutes later and headed to her closet. Finding something quick to throw on, she came back in some Minnie Mouse short pajamas and slid underneath the covers.

"You're leaving?" she asked me.

"You want me to?"

She shook her head. Taking my clothes off, I slid under the covers with her and turned the light off.

"Tell me something that I don't know about you. Not Mace or Maceo, but about De'Maceo."

"I have a hard time letting people in. Only person I care for more than you is my brother. I don't know who my pops is, and my mama a crack addict. She used to sell us as kids and buy us back. When I was twelve, she got so high that she burned down our entire apartment complex. Luckily, we made it out alive. I haven't seen her since the day I turned twelve. I've been doing everything in my power to make sure my brother and I lived good."

"Wow! So where is your mom?"

"I'm going to be honest. I don't know, and I don't give a fuck. If I come across her, I might just kill her."

"So, you and Mario are nine months apart? Do you ever want kids?"

"Yeah, I want like five kids."

"Boy, that's a lot of kids," she said, laughing.

"I want a big-ass family. It's always been my brother and me. We had a couple of cousins we fucked with, but those niggas are jealous. They always had more than us, but because we hustle hard to get what we want, the hate just increased."

"I don't think it's hate. I think people would rather see you fail than prosper. They are afraid that you'll be more than what they are now."

I listened to her talk, and I agreed with that.

"Enough about me. What about you?"

"I've told you everything about me, although I do wanna admit, I don't think my parents are actually my parents."

"Why you assume that?"

"The way they treat me. I don't have any proof because I look like my brother, but I don't think they are my parents. They leave me here for weeks at a time with enough food and drinks and a little money, but my little sister told me that they have another house in the south suburbs, and I found that odd because I had no idea about it."

"What the fuck? What type of shit is that? But it's alright, though. As long as we together, I got you. I know you said they were preachers and professors, but I don't give a fuck. If they do some shit to you, I expect to know about it. Long as I'm around, I got you."

"You don't have to do that, Mace. I'm good for now. If I need anything, I'll ask you." She yawned.

"Hell nah! If I see it, I'ma get it for you, simple as that," I said to her, but I didn't hear anything. She was knocked out.

Laying back on the pillow, I stared at the ceiling before I realized that I fucked around and fell in love.

Chapter 6

Erian

Two Years Later . . .

It was Mario's and my two-year anniversary, and I was excited. We had grown as a couple, and life was treating us good, but I couldn't help but feel like a storm was brewing between us. Lately, I'd been feeling like he was hiding something from me. I couldn't accuse him of cheating because I had no proof of that. Nothing he was doing gave any indication that he was doing something.

I was getting dressed up in the outfit I had bought for our anniversary celebration. Putting on my all-black lingerie set, my man's favorite color, then the dress that I had delivered two weeks ago, I had to admire my curves. Mario loved my curves, and I loved him.

Glancing down at my baby bump in my dress, I knew I should've been hiding it, but we weren't in Chicago, so no one knew us here, and I knew we weren't taking pictures like that. And if we did, Mario would surely hide it.

Hearing him come into the room, I turned around quickly.

"Damn! Thick in all the right places. What my son doing?" he asked, walking over and rubbing my stomach. That little boy started moving all over the place. I couldn't deal with these two.

"Move, De'Marrion. You always come and get him riled up. Leave him be."

"Awww! You jealous I pay more attention to him than your nappy-head self. It's okay. Daddy love you too," he said, wrapping his arms around me.

"You ready to enjoy our night? I got something nice planned for us," I told him.

"Hell yes. If it ends with you bouncing on this dick, I'm down for whatever."

I muffed him, then walked around, grabbed my jacket, and headed out of the room with him behind me.

I had planned a trip for us to Watch Hill, Rhode Island, to the beautiful Ocean House resort, where I rented the Beach Stone suite that was on the beach. The view was beautiful. Mario thought that we were leaving, but we were really going to the patio, where I hired us a private chef who had prepared a meal from a menu I had asked for.

"Why are we coming back here?" Turning the corner, he stopped short and looked at me. "You did all this shit for us?" he asked.

"Of course I did. Now, come on." I grabbed his hand, and we walked to the table.

Pulling my chair out for me, he waited until I sat down, then pushed me up to the table before going to sit down.

"Damn! Thank you, ma. I ain't never been nowhere this nice before. I appreciate this shit," he said sincerely.

"You deserve it, Mario. Since we've been together, you've made me the happiest woman ever. You showed me things that nobody ever could. No matter what came your way, you talked to me about it and made decisions that included me. Now, I'm having your first child, and I can't help but feel overjoyed because I know you love him as much as me. I just wish you would see that you're just as great as I see you. I love you, De'Marrion Perkins."

"I love you too, ma. And I'ma always go hard for my family. You know this. Since you came in my life, you've made everything better. Nothing stood in our way, and we've been a team. I want this shit forever with you and him. I promise to grind non-stop to protect y'all and provide for y'all," he said, leaning across the table and placing a kiss on my lips.

That one kiss turned into a deep, passionate-filled one. Hearing somebody clear their throat, I saw the waiters and the chef.

"Madame, the food you have requested awaits. Would you like it now or served a little later?"

"Now is fine, Javier. I want to thank you for preparing this meal for us. I've left your tip with the payment. Enjoy yourself with it."

"Thank you, honey. Now, if you need anything else, you have my number," Javier said before instructing them to place our food down and removing the cover. They walked away and came back with our drinks.

"Enjoy your meals," the servers said and walked away.

"Damn, you went all out. Porterhouse steak, lobster tail, loaded baked potatoes, and roasted chicken. A nigga about to eat good. Bow your head, girl." He prayed over our food before we dove in and started eating.

After dinner, we took a walk on the beach, and I had another surprise for him. I didn't know how he was going to react to it. As we walked farther, we saw roses that led us to the boat. He looked at me, and I just smiled at him as I leaned into his side and pulled us in the direction of the boat.

There was a man waiting for us. "Erian and Mario, I presume? I'm Bryce, your captain for today."

"Yeah, man, the name is De'Marrion. Baby, what are we doing here?" He looked at me curiously.

"I just wanted us to end our night perfectly, and what better way to end it than a relaxing trip into the water?"

"Are you guys ready?"

"Yeah, we ready, man. But can you be careful? She's pregnant with my son."

"I understand, son. Got one on the way myself. I'll be extra careful," he said to Mario as he helped me up the stairs.

I looked around the boat and was amazed at its size and coziness. I sat on one of the benches, and Mario came and sat next to me.

"You did all this shit for me, and all I got you was this," he said.

"Got me what?" I asked, turning to look at him, and he was down on one knee.

"No! Unh-uh, De'Marrion. Quit playing."

He kept the smile on his face the entire time. "You already know I ain't playing. I ain't gotta give you a long speech because you already know where I stand with you. We've been through everything from this gun case I just beat to my son you are carrying in your stomach. I wouldn't be where I'm at now if you hadn't put up with me. I love you, Erian, and I can't see my life without you and my son, man. Just say you'll marry a nigga."

"Yes, I'll marry you! Ahhhh! I can't believe this," I yelled out as he slipped the ring on my finger. Pulling him into a hug, I kissed him on the lips.

"Aye, they got a place we can go on the boat?"

I shrugged my shoulders, but I asked Bryce. "Hey, Bryce, is there a place that I can use the restroom?"

"Sure thing, baby doll. Through that door in front of you and to the left."

"Thank you." Grabbing Mario's hand, I pulled him with me. In the bathroom, I pulled my panties down and my dress up.

"I swear you better not make one sound," I told him, as he got behind me and slid in.

"Mmmm!" I moaned out.

"Damn, this pussy wet," he groaned out.

I was already horny, but him proposing made it worse.

"If I find out another nigga so much as sniffed it, I'm bodying him," he chastised as I threw it back on him. The thing was, Mario talked a lot of shit, but I usually had him tapping out quick as hell.

"Fuck! Throw that shit back. Look at all that ass jiggle," he said, smacking it.

I looked over my shoulder at him. He was biting his bottom lip as I tightened my pussy muscles around him, continuing to throw it back, making my ass cheeks clap just a li'l bit.

"Fuck! Damn, you about to make me nut. Slow down."

Ignoring him, I backed him against the door frame and bent over just a little so he could go deeper.

"Erian! Fuck, slow down," he said, catching my hips and guiding me slowly as he delivered deep strokes.

"Oh my God! Mario!"

"Don't 'oh my God, Mario' nothin'. I told yo' ass to slow down," he said, pounding into me with no mercy.

"I'm cumming," I yelled out.

"Fuckkkkk! Me too," he gritted out as we released together.

Falling back against the door frame, he pulled me back with him. "I'm not fucking with you no mo'. I done missed my ride."

"We have it for a next for couple of hours. Let's get cleaned up and head back up there."

Fixing our clothes, we cleaned ourselves before we went back up the stairs. The sun was slowly setting, and we watched it go down.

His phone vibrated, and he hit the ignore button. I found that odd. He never did that. I would just chalk it up to us spending time together.

For the remainder of the night, we watched the sunset, walked back up the beach again, and finally returned to our suite.

Two Weeks Later . . .

Mario had been acting strange since we returned. I didn't know what was going on, but I was surely about to find out. Pulling up to him and Mace's townhouse, I noticed an additional car there. Getting out, I headed to the door and rang the doorbell. I heard talking, then the door opening, and a female stood before me. Not wanting to jump to conclusions, I asked if she could get Mario. She called for Mario, and he came to the door.

"What's up, ma? What are you doing here?" he asked, stepping out on the porch, closing the door.

"Well, I've been calling for the last hour or so and didn't get any answer, so I decided to stop by being that you missed our appointment and you haven't missed one yet. I was concerned. You've been acting weird for the last couple of weeks. What's going on?"

"Damn! My fault, ma. I was busy getting some shit ready, and it slipped my mind. I ain't even hear my phone go off. Did you reschedule?" He grabbed his phone out of his pocket.

"It was dead, bae. My fault."

I just looked at him. "Who is ol' girl who came to the door, Mario?"

"Amaya? Oh, she ain't nobody. She's helping Mace and I with something. Did you reschedule?" he asked again.

"Yeah, tomorrow at twelve. Why are we standing out here and not inside?"

"It ain't safe in there for you. I'm about to get ready for work anyways. I'll come through when I get off." He kissed me on the cheek and rushed back inside.

I looked at the door and went back to my car. Once I got inside, I cried. I didn't know what I had done, and it made it even worse that she came out right behind me, and he kissed her on the lips. Well, it looked like the lips, but it could've been her cheek. She walked off to her car, got in, and pulled off.

After finally getting myself under control, I drove home and got in the bed. I was exhausted from hiding that I was pregnant and the crying I had done.

My phone pinged. Grabbing it, I saw it was a message from Facebook.

Mona: I'm going to need you to stay away from Mario. He doesn't want you, and y'all haven't been together in the longest. No need for you to still be contacting him.

I had to read the message twice to make sure that I wasn't tripping. Screenshotting it, I sent it to Mario. A few minutes later, he called my phone.

Answering it, I spoke into the phone. "Mario, who the fuck is this bitch?"

"I was about to ask you the same fucking thing. I don't know who that bitch is. I haven't been messing with no bitch but you since we got together. So, whoever the fuck she is, I don't know. And you better not be stressing over a bitch I don't know. You are carrying my fucking son."

"Are you cheating on me, De'Marrion? Just tell me. I promise I won't be mad," I cried.

"When do I have time to cheat on yo' ass? I don't have time. I spend the majority, if not all my time, with you.

From there, I go to work and back to you. I don't have time to cheat, so don't even start with that shit."

"Whatever. So who is she?"

"Didn't I just fucking tell you that I don't know? I haven't been with no bitch. I've been to work, with Maceo, and to you. You tweaking, Erian. Get some rest and don't stress out my son."

I sighed as he hung up the phone. I thought about what he said, and it made sense. Laying down in the bed, I took a nap. I didn't have shit else to do. School was out for the day, and I didn't have to work if I didn't want to. My father had died and left me more than enough money. My mother didn't want the money, so she relinquished it over to me, so my son was going to be well taken care of. I wished I could tell my mama, but I knew she would be disappointed, so I'd wait until I was a month from my due date, then tell her.

Fluffing my pillow, I closed my eyes and drifted to sleep.

"Erian! Erian! Shorty, wake up!" was all I heard as Mario tried shaking me awake. I felt his hand between my legs and a cramp in my lower stomach. Sitting up, I looked up at him, and he had a look of panic on his face.

"Bae, get up. We gotta go to the ER."

"What's wrong?"

I looked down at my bed, and it was soaked in blood. A sharp pain shot across my stomach, and I howled in pain.

"Bae, I think I'm losing him," I said to him through the pain.

"Naw, don't say that shit. Come on. I'll carry you." He picked me up and brought me to his car.

He drove me to Christ, since that was the hospital I was supposed to deliver him at. Pulling up into the ER, he went inside and came back with a wheelchair. I opened the car door as best I could, and he helped me into the wheelchair.

The nurses immediately sent me up to the maternity floor. I was scared and didn't want to lose my son. I knew if I hadn't been stressing, none of this would've happened to him.

The nurse wheeled me into the room, and Mario picked me up and placed me in the bed.

"Can you help her undress? The doctor will be in here shortly. After you get her undressed, can you get me from the hallway so that I can put this on to monitor the baby?" the nurse said.

Mario nodded his head, and she left. I couldn't stop crying as he helped me get undressed. There was so much blood. I prayed that it was something wrong with me and not him, but I hadn't felt him move since earlier today.

"Stop crying, ma. Everything gon' be alright."

"I don't think it is. Why haven't I felt him move? Why hasn't he moved?" I asked Mario hysterically.

"Erian, calm down, bae. Please."

I started to calm down some.

"Hi, Erian. I heard that you were having some bleeding. We are going to get your vitals as we hook you up to the monitor to check the baby's heart rate."

They placed the fetal doppler around me, and I looked at Mario. He was staring at the screen. I heard the heartbeat, and I breathed a sigh of relief.

"I told you, ma, I told you he was going to be good."

The doctor and nurse sat off to the side and were looking at the chart, but when I saw the line of his heartbeat drop, I knew something wasn't right.

"Erian, we have to get you to surgery. We're going to perform a C-section. His heart rate has dropped tremendously, and it's imperative that we take him out. They are going to prep you for surgery now. I'll see you in a few," my doctor said.

I looked at Mario, and he looked at me.

"Okay, thank you," I lay back in the bed and prayed that the baby came out alright. I wouldn't know what to do without him.

"Erian, whatever happens, know I love you, ma. Know I want a life with both of y'all. He's going to be alright. I promise," he said, but I could hear the uncertainty in his voice.

"I love you too, De'Marrion. What if he doesn't make it? What if they ask you to choose between us?" I asked, letting the tears fall down my face.

"I'm choosing you, ma. I can create another kid, but I can't create another you. I can't do that, bae. I can't lose you, too," he told me.

I nodded my head because I understood where he was coming from.

"Erian, we are here to take you for the surgery. Sir, if you want to be in the room, you can, but we ask that you allow the doctor to do his job. If an emergency comes up, we will ask you to leave. Do you understand?" Mario nodded his head. "You can follow Tiffany to the room to get suited in. She's in good hands, son."

Mario nodded his head, gave me a kiss, and followed behind the girl.

We left the room and went into an operating room. I was nervous, but they told me not to be. They prepped me for everything, and before I knew it, Mario was at my side and the doctor was getting ready to start cutting.

"How is his heart rate?" he asked.

"It's stable, sir, but it's still not out of dangerous territory. We need to get him out," I heard the nurse say.

"Erian, do you want to be awake for this?"

I nodded.

"Alright, let's get ready."

I looked at Mario. I wanted to reach out and wipe the tears that had fallen, but I couldn't because I was restrained.

"Why are you crying?" I asked him.

"I'm good, ma," he said, wiping the tears.

"Okay, Erian, you're going to feel a lot of pressure, and then it'll be over."

"Okay."

I felt the pressure he was talking about, then it was gone. Mario looked at me before looking on the other side of the sheet.

"Mario, can you see him?" I asked.

He nodded his head, and I heard movement, and then a bunch of stuff being called out.

"What's wrong, Mario? Is my baby alright?" I asked him, but he refused to look at me.

"His umbilical cord is wrapped around his neck, and he isn't breathing."

"What you mean he isn't breathing? What the hell is going on?" I tried to pull in my restraints and sit up.

"Ma'am, calm down, or we will have to put you to sleep," the nurse said, pressing on my shoulder.

"I don't give a fuck! What is going on with my son? Is he alright?" I yelled out.

"Call the time of death."

Time of death? I repeated in my head. It couldn't have been what they were saying.

"He's gone, ma," Mario said, and I just looked at him. He couldn't have been telling me what I think he was. My baby wasn't dead.

"What you mean he's gone?" I cried out. I couldn't believe this. It wasn't true. My baby boy wasn't gone.

"Time of death, 4:44 a.m., June 26, 2011."

"No!" I cried out as Mario laid his head on mine.

He couldn't have been gone. Not my baby. I couldn't believe it. He was gone. Trying to get the restraints off, I felt the nurses holding me down. A nice, cold sedative flowed through my veins, and I just looked at Mario. I couldn't believe this was the end of my beginning with my son.

Chapter 7

Mario

It had been two months since the death of my son, and Erian refused to talk to me. Even though the fault was neither of ours, she blamed me for our son dying, and I wanted to smack the fuck outta her. Her insecurity was driving a wedge between us. She knew I wouldn't fucking cheat on her, and I wished she would understand that I wasn't no cheating-ass nigga. Some bitch messages her, and suddenly, I'm cheating on her.

I looked at her as she lay in bed. Her mother had gone to work, and her stepfather was sleeping until he had to go to work that night. He drove trucks. I was trying to get her to talk to me so I could find out what was wrong, but she insisted on ignoring me.

"Erian, you know I gotta go to work in a few. We need to talk."

"Go to work then. I don't feel like talking."

"You don't feel like doing a fucking thing nowadays. I know it's hard on you, bae, but that shit hard on me, too. You act like I did the shit. It wasn't my fault."

"It was your fault! Had you not forgot about the fucking appointment, I would've been able to see if my fucking son was alright. Instead, you were busy with some bitch," she screamed, sitting up in bed.

"That bitch was planning your fucking surprise wedding, but fuck it now. Yo' ass is too insecure. I'm not yo' fucking daddy, and you need to see that shit. I haven't cheated on you, nor put my hands on you, so stop comparing me to him. I ain't given you a fucking indication that I was cheating on you. You let these bitches who don't want shit but to be in yo' spot tell you shit. I haven't fucked a bitch, looked at bitch, nor been with another bitch since I've been with you. Two fucking years I've been with you. Have I ever given you an inkling that I was cheating on your dumb ass?"

She sat there quietly.

"Exactly what I fucking thought. Every bitch who speak to me, look my way, or acknowledge me doesn't want me, and you need to get it through your head. Everybody around us is moving on with their lives, but you are so hell bent on blaming me for something that wasn't my fault. Yes, I lost track of time, and yes, I fucked up, but I was the one who held him on my chest until they took him away. I'm the one who did the arrangements for him. I'm the one who watched him take his first and last breath. You don't think that shit is hard? I had to watch my fucking son die. You so fucking selfish, you haven't asked how the fuck I felt. All because you blame me for something that wasn't my fault," I snapped at her ass.

I could feel the tears coming down my face, but I didn't give a fuck. Erian had me fucked up. Her selfish ass didn't give a fuck about what I was going through. Nobody knew about the baby because she wanted to keep the shit a secret. I couldn't even fucking tell my brother, and that shit was eating me up on the inside. I rarely kept anything from him, but out of respect for my woman, I did just that. She had both of us suffering in silence, and all I wanted to do was get that shit off my chest.

"Mario, I'm sorry. I didn't know you felt like that. I'm sorry. It's just hard knowing my baby boy didn't even get to see life and enjoy it. I'm just . . . I don't know what to do or how I feel," she said, wrapping her arms around my shoulders.

I rubbed my hand up and down her arm as she cried. I didn't know what the fuck to do, but I knew I had to get ready for work.

"Look, ma, I'll come back over after work. Get some sleep. Relax, and we can talk about it later."

"Alright, Mario. If I come up there and that bitch is in your face again, it's going to be a problem. I'm so fucking serious," she yelled at me.

Pushing her ass off me, I got up and mugged her. "So, it's fuck what I was just talking about, huh? You steady worried about bitches. They either want to break us up or fuck me. You be worried about the wrong shit. We got bigger shit to worry about than some bitches wanting me," I snapped at her ass as I grabbed my work shirt off the floor.

I felt air swing past my face. Standing up straight, I saw Erian mugging me, fist clenched at her side.

"Don't put yo' fucking hands on me. I haven't hit you, so don't fucking hit me." Bending down, I slipped my feet in my shoes, and I felt Erian hitting me in the back of my head.

"Stop, Erian!" I said, pushing her back. She ran back up on me and tried hitting me in the face, but I blocked her ass and pushed her back. Her next move sealed the deal for us. She drew back and punched me in the nose. With quick reflexes, I smacked her ass back, and she landed on the floor. Looking down at her as my nose dropped with blood, I wish she was a nigga, because I would've fucked her up.

"I'm done! We are fucking done. The wedding and engagement is fucking off. Yo' insecure ass is allowing a bitch that I don't even know to get in yo' head. I bet that's that bitch sending you shit about me even though I'm right here with you. You so fucking gullible and weak. I'm good on you. I hope the next nigga can fix what I couldn't," I yelled at her before I left out her fucking room and out the front door.

I meant everything I said to her. Erian was too damaged from her fucked up parents. I had never hit her before that, but those were reflexes. I still felt fucked up about hitting her. No matter how many times she hit me, I should've never hit her back. Looking at my face in the mirror, I knew I couldn't fucking go to work like this, and I was going to lose money, but it wasn't shit I could do. Closing the visor, I turned the car on and headed home.

Chapter 8

Saiyah

Staring down at the stick in my hand, I couldn't believe that I had gotten myself in this situation. As much as I loved Maceo, there was no way that I could go through with this. A baby just wasn't on my agenda at the age of nineteen. This just couldn't be life. With a heavy sigh, I tossed the pregnancy test into the trash can right before grabbing my phone and calling Planned Parenthood.

"Hi, I wanted to make an appointment for an abortion," I stated when the receptionist answered. A tear slid down my face. Getting this abortion was going to take everything in me, but I knew it was for the best. I was barely an adult. After giving them all my information, I had an appointment. I didn't believe in abortion not one bit, but I couldn't allow Maceo to destroy my life. On top of that, I hadn't graduated high school yet and still lived with my parents.

Speaking of parents, they would be home soon. I got up and startred straightening up my room. I was vacuuming the floor when I heard my phone vibrating. Picking it up, I saw that it was Maceo. Rolling my eyes, I answered the phone.

"Hello," I said, and I heard a bunch of commotion in the background.

"Hellllllll-O!" I said, and his voice finally came through the phone.

"Yo, what's up, baby? What you doing?"

"Nothing, Maceo, just straightening up my room before my parents get here."

"Oh, a'ight. You don't have anything to tell me, do you?"

I pulled the phone from my ear and looked at it suspiciously.

"No. Why would you ask that?"

"I'm only asking because I see you just received an email from Planned Parenthood."

"What the fuck? Why are you logged into my emails and shit, Mace?" I asked. I was low-key pissed that he was even connected to my shit, but then I remembered that when my phone died one day, I logged into my accounts on his phone. Now, I was kicking my own ass for not logging out.

"Fuck all that hot shit you spitting, Yah. What the fuck yo' ass going to Planned Parenthood for in the first place? You pregnant, Yah?"

I rolled my eyes at his question. I didn't want to lie to him, so I decided to tell the truth. "Yeah, I'm pregnant, Mace, but I can't keep this baby. I have my whole life ahead of me to be tied down with a baby," I said quietly through my sadness. Even though that was the truth and I was scared to get the abortion, but I had to do it.

"So, it's just fuck how I feel, huh?"

"Mace, what can we do with a baby? You still doing your job as a janitor, and I'm still in school. We're going to be struggling. I want to give my baby the best," I stated with finality.

"Man, you know what, Saiyah? You right, baby. Do what you think is best. I'm done," he said, and I heard the phone signaling that he had hung up.

Sighing, I set my phone down and continued to clean up. Then I heard the infamous ding from a text message coming through.

Mace: It's fucked up how low you think of me. I grind day in and day out to help you, but yo' ass still finds a way to be unappreciative. Get the abortion but understand that I don't want shit else to do with you if you do. Obviously, you've made up your mind for the both of us. I love you, Yah, and I wish you the best of luck.

I went to get the abortion a few days later, but I couldn't go through with it. Erian and I walked out with some prenatal pills and some condoms. I feared being a mom, but I was more scared of getting the abortion. I just couldn't do it, no matter how much I tried to talk myself into it.

I felt Erian tap me. Looking up, I saw Maceo, and I could've shitted bricks. The look on his face let me know he was pissed off and disgusted with me. Instead of saying anything, I tried to hand him the sonogram, but he smacked it on the ground.

"Mace, I—"

"Yo, you grimy as fuck. Why the fuck would you do that? Huh? You knew how much I wanted fucking kids, and you go get rid of my seed."

"But Mace, I di—"

"I don't give a fuck about your reasons. You real fucked up for that, Yah. You bogus as fuck, man. Fuck you, Saiyah. And you too, Erian, for being here with her."

With each word he said, my heart broke. I was trying to tell him that I didn't do it, but he kept cutting me off.

"Fuck you too, Maceo. You and your bitch-ass brother. Fuck both of y'all. If you would've listened to her, you would know that she did —"

He cut Erian off before she could finish her sentence. I had never witnessed Maceo in such rare form.

"I'm out. Have a good life, both of y'all," he said solemnly before turning around and hopping in his car. Closing the door, he smashed outta the parking lot.

Bending down, I picked up the sonogram of our baby. I was three months and two days pregnant. I was going to give him some breathing room before I tried to tell him again. Hopefully, he would listen next time.

After multiple times of trying to contact Maceo, I decided to just pop up on him. He had blocked me on everything, so I couldn't get in contact with him. Even Mario wasn't messing with me. Getting off the bus two blocks from their townhome, I walked all the way to his house. I had Erian on the phone as I walked toward my destination.

"Saiyah, I don't think you should go over there." Erian begged me not to go as I approached his door.

"I'm already here." Knocking on the door, I listened to Erian beg me to leave, but I couldn't, so I hung up on her.

I heard the door unlocking and the knob turning. When the door swung open, I couldn't believe what I was seeing. There was a woman standing there in the shirt I got Maceo for his twenty-second birthday. I wanted to cuss her out, but it wasn't about her. This was about Maceo, myself, and our unborn child.

"Um, can I help you?" the woman asked.

"Yes, I'm looking for Maceo. Is he available?"

"Yeah, one second. Maceo, there's some young girl at your door."

I rolled my eyes at the bitch. I heard voices, then Maceo appeared at the door.

"What's up, Yah?" he said coldly.

"Um, can we talk in private? I wanted to talk to you about something."

"Nah, we ain't got shit to talk about. You aborted my child when I begged you not to. That's fucked up, Yah."

"Maceo, just let me explain," I told him, but the girl cut me off.

"Maceo, hurry up, daddy. I'm waiting on you."

He looked back at me, and I swiped the tears that had fallen down my face.

"What was you saying now?" he asked nonchalantly. I knew he saw the tears but didn't care. The De'Maceo that I was staring at wasn't the one I had fallen in love with over the last two years.

"Nothing. Bye, Maceo." I turned around and walked back to the bus stop. It was no use talking to him. Whatever we had was now dead and over. Looking down at my stomach that was slightly poking out, I rubbed it and promised my baby that we were going to be ok with or without Maceo in our lives.

Chapter 9

Erian

Six Years Later . . .

Walking through the doors of Keller and Co., the law firm where I worked, I saw Mrs. Keller standing at the front desk, and I wanted to walk out of this depressing-ass place I called work. Taking a deep breath, I spoke to everyone before proceeding over to my desk and placing my purse in the drawer. Sitting down, I grabbed the folder with the day's instructions and client list, then turned the phones on. As I listened to the voicemails that were left, I wrote them down and took all the necessary steps to make appointments and email the information that was needed.

After I was done, I got ready for the first client of the day. While creating the new files, I looked up at the door and couldn't believe who I was seeing. De'Marrion Perkins had just walked through the door. Panicking, I hid under the desk as if I were looking for something. I prayed that he would go over to Saiyah's desk, but that was all short-lived when I heard the tapping on the top of my desk.

Raising my head, I looked up, and I couldn't help but stare at his beautiful face.

"Um, how may I help you?"

"Yeah. I got a nine o'clock appointment with Mr. Keller. Is he in yet?"

"Yes, he is. You're De'Marrion Perkins, am I correct?"

"Man, Erian, quit that shit. You know who the fuck I am." His voice got louder. I looked at him with a raised eyebrow, and I guess he realized he was too loud.

"My fault. You are talking all professional and shit when you know I'm not used to that shit."

"Well, I'm at work, and I stopped being ghetto and loud years ago. But as I was saying, you're De'Marrion Perkins, correct?"

"Yeah, that's me, ma," he said, licking his lips at me. I ignored him, and he continued to stare at me.

"Ugh, De'Marrion, why did you tell me that the appointment was at nine thirty when I got an email confirmation for nine?" a woman said as she was approaching him. She was beautiful, and I could tell that she was expecting from the round bump in her stomach.

"Man, Tee, cut all that rah-rah noise that you are making, sweetheart. Where is Maceo at?"

I looked over at Saiyah, and she looked nervous at the mention of Maceo.

"He's on his way in with Li'l Maceo. Why?"

"Bye, Tee. You loud as hell." Turning his attention back to me, he asked if there was anything else that he needed.

Grabbing the folder with his name on it, I handed it to him and told him to have a seat. Reaching down in the drawer, I grabbed my phone and saw Saiyah had messaged me.

Saiyah: I'm going to the bathroom. Let me know when Maceo is gone.

Looking at her, I nodded. She hurriedly got up and left out. Shortly after, I saw Maceo come in with a li'l boy who looked exactly like him.

"Yo, is dude ready?" Maceo asked De'Marrion.

"Nah, I think shorty went to check."

Excusing myself, I knocked on the door. "Mr. Keller, your nine o'clock appointment is here. Should I tell them to come in, or would you like me to set up the conference room?"

"You can instruct them to come back. How many are out there?"

"Three adults: two men and one woman. And there is a child. He looks to be about two or three. Is that alright?"

"Yes, yes! Have them come on," he said. Mrs. Keller, on the other hand, didn't look too pleased.

"Ok, sir. I'll send them back."

When I walked back to the front, they stood up.

"Mr. Keller will see you now. Follow me." I walked back to the office, nervous and praying that Maceo and Saiyah wouldn't see each other.

I ushered them into the office. After everyone was inside, I made a beeline for the bathroom door.

"Saiyah, bring yo' ass out here."

"Are they gone?"

"No, Saiyah, they aren't gone. You can't avoid Maceo forever. What about Macayla? You not going to let him meet her or her know who her dad is?"

"I'm just not ready to deal with Maceo."

"Whatever. Just to let you know, his baby mother is out there, too. I think you should get back to your desk. Christina look like she on some bullshit."

"I hate that bitch. I can't wait until I find a new job. Travis don't pay us enough to deal with his wife."

"I swear he don't, but let's get back out there."

As we were walking out, Christina was heading our way with a scowl on her face. "Is there a reason that you two aren't at your desks?"

"Yes, we were using the restroom. A personal hygiene issue occurred, and I was helping a co-worker. Is that an issue?"

"Actually, it is. The phones were ringing, and no one was there to answer them."

I side-eyed her. We had been working there longer than she had been an adult. If that phone rang, we would've heard it.

"Mrs. Keller, I apologize. It was my fault. My monthly started, and I didn't have any personal hygiene materials to handle it, so I asked her for them, but the clients walked in, and it was stalled. It's my fault, and it won't happen again."

"Oh, it better not, or you'll be looking for a new job. Return to your desk. When those guys leave, please make copies of the documents they sign and file them. Thank you," she said with an attitude.

"Bitch," I mumbled when she was far away.

Grabbing my arm, Saiyah pulled me back out front. Sitting at her desk, she got to work, and I relaxed as I went through the email requests from Keller's website. An hour had passed before they emerged from the office. Tee looked as though she had been crying, Maceo looked pissed, and De'Marrion looked irritated.

Maceo was on his way to my desk when he noticed Saiyah. I held my breath, but nothing prepared me for the words that came out of his mouth.

"What the fuck is this, Yah? Is that my fucking daughter?" he asked, staring at something behind her desk.

Saiyah looked over at me, and I knew I couldn't save her from Maceo, but I could help the situation.

"Maceo, now isn't the time for this conversation. We work here, and you could get us fired. If you want to talk to her, we get off at six, but please leave before she loses her job," I said.

He looked at her, but Saiyah wouldn't look him in the face.

"Yeah, a'ight. Tee, make the fucking appointment. I'm in the car. Can't believe this shit," he spat as he walked out of the door.

I looked at Saiyah to make sure she was going to be alright before going back to my desk

"I'm sorry about that. What is the return date for Mr. Keller?" I asked.

"The twenty-third of July. But what do you know about the girl right over there? Is that little girl really Maceo's?"

I ignored her questions. She didn't need to know about Saiyah or Macayla.

"The only available time is four in the afternoon. Is that alright?" I asked, plastering a fake smile on my face.

"Yes, that's fine, and that must be your li'l friend. It's okay. Let her know it's only one woman in Maceo's life, and it ain't her."

"Shit, it ain't you either. That nigga dumped you before Li'l Mace was born, and y'all was only fucking. Take yo' ass to the car." De'Marrion, or Mario as I called him, said then approached Saiyah after ol' girl left out with an attitude.

I couldn't hear what he was saying, but Saiyah continuously nodding her head made me calm down a little. After they talked, she got up and hugged him as he walked past me out the door.

I looked over at her, and she just waved me off, telling me that she was good. I sat back down at my desk and stored the files that they had left and waited for our next appointment of the day.

Chapter 10

Maceo

For the second time that day, a female seemed to piss me off. The first time was Tee's stupid ass when I found that her ass had about fifteen grams of crack on her and that shit was like a life sentence to a nigga. Why the fuck she even had the shit in the first place was what had me puzzled. Now her stupid ass was hit with possession of a controlled substance with the intent to sell. So now, she might have to sit down for 4–15 years with a possibility of probation, and I had to pay a fucking $250,000 fine because her broke ass couldn't afford the shit. Then, she wanna cry about the shit because she got caught. Tee was already pregnant, so why she had crack was still questionable, and I had every intention of finding out why.

When I went in the office and saw Erian, I had no clue that Saiyah worked there, too. I thought I saw her, but I just knew my mind was playing tricks on me. Then, when Christina said her name, I knew that it was shorty I had seen. A part of me was pissed that she was hiding from me after she pulled that stunt. But when I walked out that office and saw that big-ass picture of a little girl who looked like my son, I got pissed. That shit conjured up so many feelings inside of a nigga.

Back in the day, Saiyah was a nigga's heart, and even though I knew I shouldn't have been fucking with her young ass, everything about her drew me in. For a seventeen-year-old, she was stacked in all the right places, and I had to be the nigga to stake claim on pussy that I hadn't been seen or touched. At first, it was about smashing and dipping, but after I got to know her, I realized I started falling for her, and I couldn't stop. Shit was good, until I got word that somebody saw her in the abortion clinic.

My ass flew down to that place, but by the time I got there, she was walking out the clinic with her li'l prescription bag, all hunched over, with Erian helping her as she cried. The look on my face must've had her ass shook because she tried to explain and even handed me something, but I smacked that shit on the ground. Saiyah had me fucked up. Dirty or not, I knew she wasn't on birth control. Yet and still, I nutted inside her every chance I got. Yeah, I tried to trap her, and from what I just saw, that shit had worked.

I couldn't say she didn't try to get in contact with me because she did. I would ignore her calls, texts, and voicemails. I didn't have social media accounts, so she could never message or post on my wall about it. And when she came to my crib, I had a new bitch already. Had I known she was trying to tell me that she didn't abort my baby, we probably would've been together, but wasn't shit I could do about it now.

Glancing in the rearview mirror, I saw Li'l Mace knocked the fuck out. Looking up, I saw Tee walking toward me with a scowl on her face.

"So, you got another baby? Who is that bitch, Maceo? So, Li'l Mace has a little sister?"

I looked at Teriana like she was crazy. She had me fucked up.

"Last I checked, I was a grown-ass man and didn't have to answer to you. Secondly, don't worry about where my dick goes. It ain't in you, and that's all you need to know. And she's older than Li'l Mace."

The door opened, and my brother slid in the front seat. He looked back at Tee ass with a mug. "You always starting some shit. Yo' suburban ass gon' get that ass beat one day. Those two from out west and will beat yo' ass with no hesitation. Mind yo' business."

"Fuck y'all."

I looked at her ass, and she was already pissing me off. "No, fuck you, Tee. You got us in some shit that ain't got shit do with us. We don't deal nor dabble in drugs no more. We make music, and here yo' dumb ass goes getting caught up in the shit. Matter of fact, why you have the shit in the first place?" I was lying about some parts, but Tee stupid-ass didn't have to know that.

"My mother sent me to get something for her, and I didn't know I was going to get pulled over."

"You were doing seventy in a thirty-five-mile zone. What the fuck you thought was going to happen? And why you bringing yo' mother crack in the first place? Where you get it from?"

"Maceo, she can't function without it, and she sent me up on Roosevelt to get it."

"Out west? You were fucking out west in a hundred-thousand-dollar car? Are you fucking stupid? Yeah, you lucky you got caught with the crack because yo' ass could be dead. Stupid ass. Sit back so we can go home."

"Aye, bruh, take me to grab my car. I gotta pick up Chelley ass," my brother said.

"A'ight."

My brother's girlfriend, Chelley, hated me. She swore I knew why Mario wouldn't fuck with her like that, but that was between my brother and me. I didn't have to tell that bitch shit. I knew where his heart really was, and she wasn't it. If she didn't know what they had was over, then I didn't know what to tell her. His ass didn't even sleep in the same bed as her. That nigga spent more time at his condo in the city than at the house he bought them in the suburbs. I just hoped that now he knew where his heart was and that he went get her like I was going to get mine. It was just a matter of timing.

Chapter 11

Saiyah

I was nervous about Maceo coming back to pick me up. The only reason I had agreed was because Mario begged me to, and everyone knew I had a soft spot for him. He'd always been like a little brother to me. Mario was older than me, but I called him my little brother because he was always being childish toward me. Whenever he came around, he did something childish.

Shutting down the computer and locking up, I walked outside and waited for Maceo. I didn't have to wait long before a black and gold Maybach pulled up. The window rolled down, and I saw him.

"Bring yo' ass on, girl. It's cold out there."

Hurriedly, I walked over to the car and slid onto the heated seats. Putting my seat belt on and looking ahead, I noticed that the car wasn't moving.

"Why are you staring at me?" I asked him.

"You know what I wanna hear, Saiyah. Don't fucking play with me. You out here struggling and couldn't let me know about my daughter. What you on, man?"

"De'Maceo, what did you want me to do? Constantly blow you up? Come over to your house and see your new bitch's face? Nah, I was good, and Macayla was, too. She never has and never will want for anything. I might not have it all now, but I will eventually, and so will my baby."

"I expected you to call me when you had her. I was under the impression that you had an abortion, so what the fuck are you talking about?"

"I handed you the sonogram outside of the clinic, and you threw it on the ground. I tried telling you multiple times, and I even told you in a voicemail. It wasn't my fault that you thought the worst of me."

"You had that little brown bag in yo' hand, and you were crying, bent over, holding your stomach, so from my experience, those are all the signs that you had one."

"No, the fuck it doesn't, stupid! I had a brown bag with condoms and prenatal pills. And I was bent over from crying. I was nineteen, entering my senior year, and three months pregnant. Come on, Maceo. You knew my home life wasn't that great with my parents, and then I was pregnant. What do you think happened to me?" I snapped at him.

"Damn, Yah Yah, I'm sorry, ma. I wish I would've listened. I done missed all this time with . . ."

"Macayla. Her name is Macayla."

"Macayla. I haven't seen her, and she don't know me. What do she know about me, Saiyah?"

"I told her that you had moved when I found out about her, and I had no way of contacting you."

He breathed a sigh of relief, but I rolled my eyes.

"You hungry, or you have to pick up Macayla?"

"She's with Erian and her mother, so I can grab me something to eat."

"Where you want to go? You know we not far from downtown. You wanna go to Grand Lux?"

"I guess that's okay. Erian doesn't mind."

"Tell me about yourself. What don't I know about you since we been outta touch all these years?"

"Well, I lost my full academic scholarship to Duke because my mother called them and told them I was a pregnant slut and didn't know who my baby father is. My father co-signed with her. The college immediately withdrew it and gave it to another person. Shortly after, they kicked me out, and I moved in with Erian and her mother. I got me a job at the local Walgreens and had it up until Mr. Keller hired Erian and me. I've been working there ever since. Everything I do revolves around Macayla. I haven't been in a relationship since you because I don't have the money nor time."

"Damn! I'm sorry about your parents. They don't see Macayla, do they?"

I shook my head.

"What you need for you and Macayla?"

"Honestly, nothing," I stated. Although I needed help, I refused to ask.

"I hate a liar, and you lying. What you need, Yah Yah?"

"We need our own place, and I don't have a car. Well, I did have one, but it broke down."

"When your next off day?"

"It's Friday. The offices are closed on the weekends. So, tomorrow and Sunday."

"Well, we're going to look for a car tomorrow, and I own a couple of buildings. You can pick one to live in with Macayla, and I'll furnish it. Now that I know about you and her, can you tell her about me? I want her to know me."

I thought about it for a minute. "Yeah, I guess so. How about you pick us up for breakfast tomorrow before we go looking for the car? And I promise to pay you back every penny, Maceo. I'll even pay you the four hundred-dollar rent that I pay to Erian's mother."

"Ok, Saiyah. Whatever you wanna do. But I was doing this to benefit Macayla. She needs a roof over her head, and you need stable transportation."

I nodded my head because I knew it was about Macayla and not me.

The rest of the drive to the Grand Lux was quiet. I listened to the music. We pulled into the parking garage, and he parked. Removing my seat belt, I got out and walked ahead of him. Getting to the elevator, I pressed the button, and he looked at me weirdly when he got there.

"Yo, where the fuck did those bruises on your arm come from?"

I pulled down my sleeves. I couldn't tell him where I got them from because he would be even more protective of Macayla and me. "Nowhere."

"Saiyah Heiress Brady, where the fuck you get those bruises? Some nigga put his hands on you?"

I dropped my head and stepped onto the elevator, but he yanked me back out.

"We aren't going any muthafuckin' place until you tell me where them fucking bruises came from."

"I can't. He'll kill me, Maceo. Please, don't!"

"Fuck that! Who is this nigga who been putting hands on you? Where my daughter be at when this shit be going on?"

"De'Maceo, I can't tell you or he'll kill me and Macayla."

He looked me dead in my eyes, and I saw them turn black.

"What the fuck did you just say? Kill who? Ain't a fucking soul on this Earth gon' touch what's mine. This is my last fucking time asking you who the nigga is, or we gon' have a muthafucking misunderstanding. Do you understand?" His voice bounced off the parking garage walls.

I nodded my head.

"Who is this nigga? I want a fucking name and address."

"Erian's stepfather, Drew. Nobody is going to believe me, Mace. I can't say anything. He's been doing it for years now. He told me he would kill me if I told anybody."

His facial expression softened but then hardened. "And you have that muthafucka around my daughter? Let's go! Right muthafuckin' now. Erian still live in the same house?"

I nodded my head.

"Let's go," he said, pulling me toward him. He helped me in the car and pulled out of the parking garage.

"Why you ain't tell nobody?"

"I don't have anybody but Erian and her mom. I didn't know how to tell her or if she would believe me."

"Well, she ain't got a choice. While you at it, call Erian and tell her to pack all my baby shit. You can pack your own. Y'all staying with me until I get y'all own shit."

I looked at him with wide eyes because I couldn't stay with him and his baby mother.

"No. We can just go to a hotel for now. I can't stay with you and your baby mama," I said with finality.

"Tee got her own crib. I don't have a woman, and what I say goes at this point."

Nodding my head, I knew I should've been trying harder to get away from him, but he threatened to kill me and my daughter, and I refused to have my baby hurt because of me.

"Get out."

I looked up, and we were at Erian's house on 76th and King Drive. He ran up the stairs and knocked on the door.

Jumping out of the car, I rushed to the door, but he had already pushed his way in.

Chapter 12

De'Marrion

Listening to Chelley bitch about me taking too long was irking my fucking nerves. She found a fucking way to the airport but couldn't find one home. I didn't have time to be dealing with her childish-ass antics. I needed to swoop through one of my artists' houses, which happened to be on 76th and King Drive across from Erian's house, and grab this loud off bro. I knew I could get my weed from anywhere, but I was hoping to see her.

Pulling up to the house, I saw a black and gold Maybach that looked like my brother's. He ain't have no reason to be down this way, but he did indicate that he was going to pick Saiyah up from work earlier, so that just may be his car.

Putting the car in park, I got ready to get out, but Chelley pulled my arm. "Where you going, De'Marrion? You know I don't like being in the ghetto."

I looked at her ass and shook my head because I grew up in this fucking ghetto, as she called it, and it used to be some good-ass people around here. I turned my nose up at her.

"Ghetto? Chelley, please shut the fuck up. I grew up in this ghetto. Maybe you shouldn't be with my ghetto ass or want this ghetto dick."

"Mario, I didn't mean it —"

"Yeah, you did, Chelley, but that's cool because soon, yo' ass gon' be living in the ghetto," I growled before pushing the car door open and getting out.

"Maceo, stop! You can't do this here," I heard a female say.

Turning around, I saw Saiyah running up the stairs. Tapping my hip, I felt my gun and ran across the street. Jogging up the stairs, I saw Maceo whooping some dude's ass. I mean, that nigga was throwing straight haymakers. I ain't seen Maceo fight like that since we were kids.

Pushing the women aside, I grabbed Maceo. He turned to swing on me, and I ducked.

"Bro, stop! Yo' daughter is watching you. Calm down and tell me what the fuck is going on. Erian, take baby girl outside to Maceo's car."

She nodded her head and left, going out the door.

"De'Maceo and De'Marrion, what the hell is going on?" Erian's mother, Erin, asked.

"Tell her, Saiyah, or I'll body this nigga now."

"I'm sorry, Ms. Erin, but Drew has been raping me since I had Macayla. I was going to tell you, but he said if I did that, he would kill me and Macayla. And I couldn't have my baby's blood be on my hands. I'm sorry."

Erin looked at Saiyah, then Drew. She walked over to Drew and pressed her feet against his balls. "Did you touch my child and threaten my granddaughter?"

"Baby, she's lying. I would never touch her." He howled in pain when she pressed her foot harder into them.

I was flinching just a little bit.

"I'ma ask you again. Did you touch my fucking child?"

"Erin, she wanted it, baby. I swear she did," he yelled out.

Maceo tried to move, but I held him tighter. Ms. Erin removed her feet, and he breathed a sigh of relief. She turned around, grabbed the vase off the table, and dropped it on his dick. That nigga's scream could be heard on the next four blocks.

Maceo broke free and went to stand over that nigga. "Shut the fuck up, nigga. You weren't screaming like that when you touched her, now, were you?"

"Freeze. Everybody put your hands up."

I turned towards the jakes with my hands up. I couldn't believe that in a few short hours, I was in some bullshit, and it was about to get even worse.

"Mario, baby, are you okay? I called the police for you."

Shaking my head, everybody looked at me. I was glad my gun was registered.

The Next Morning . . .

I was free and walking out of the station, and Chelley was waiting for me. I snatched my keys and walked right past her ass. Getting in my truck, I start it up and pulled off on her ass. She had me fucked up. She knew that we didn't call no fucking boys in blue, yet she did that shit. I swear on my son, she did that shit to spite Mace.

Speaking of him, I needed to slide by his crib. Jumping on the e-way, I drove all the way to Oak Brook. I had to make sure Erian, Saiyah, and Macayla were good. I knew Mace was good.

Pulling in the driveway, I saw Tee's car there. I shook my head because I knew it was going to be some shit. My phone rang, and I saw that it was Chelley, so I answered.

"Dc'Marrion, how could you leave me out here? I don't have a ride to get home."

"That's personal, and I could care less. Look, ma, this relationship ain't working for me no mo'. You can keep the house, even yo' accounts, but we over."

"Really, De'Marrion? You're breaking up with me over the phone? That's classy," she tried to say in a ghetto manner.

I wanted to laugh because of how she sounded, but I refrained. "I'm not trying to be fucking classy, Chelley. If you want a classy nigga, go date the fucking judge you just came back off vacation with. Yeah, I know you been cheating on me, and I honestly don't give two fucks. Do you, because we over. Now, fuck off my line." Hanging up, I headed into the house, and all I heard was arguing.

"Mace, I think we should just go to a hotel. I don't want no drama."

"Hell nah, Yah Yah! I made you a promise, and I'ma stick to it. Go get you and li'l mama dressed so we can go. Thank you for the breakfast, Erian."

"What's up, bro?" I said, dapping him up when I walked in.

"You're just going to disrespect me like that, Maceo?"

"Tee, why are you in my crib, shorty? You came to drop Li'l Mace off, and that's it. Don't worry about who the fuck I got in my shit. Just know it ain't yo' ass. Now, Li'l Mace is up in his room, and my daughter and her mother are getting ready. Get the fuck outta my shit."

"Wow! That bitch come in the picture, and that's how you gon' do me?"

"Tee, get the fuck out, yo. You have been irking my nerves since I walked in. Damn, you know he don't want you and haven't in a long time. Now, gone shorty," I said.

She looked at me, and I gave her ass that look, and she left out the door, slamming it.

"She pregnant by a whole other nigga, worrying about what the fuck I'm doing. But ain't you gon' go talk to your girl?" Maceo asked me.

"Erian ain't thinking about me."

He looked at me with that look. "Nigga, those two were talking last night after everything was over and done with. Erian was thinking about you. And what the fuck took you so long getting out?"

"That stupid bitch Chelley li'l boyfriend wanted to have a talk with me. I don't got time for that bitch."

"And she too green. She called the police on yo' ass, another thing I had to do damage control on," Mace said.

"Where was them niggas Kent and Tim at? They supposed to be my fucking eyes and ears," I asked.

"Man, I hear you, but them niggas was caught up in a homicide at one of the houses. I'm trying to figure out why we didn't get no call about it, though."

"I'ma give them to the end of today to give me a call about it before I step in. You know how we do."

I shook up with him before I went into the kitchen, and he went up the stairs to get ready.

"What's up, ma? Is there some food left?" I asked Erian as I sat at the counter.

"Yeah, I put you a plate in the oven. Did you want me to get it?"

"Yeah, you can go ahead."

She walked over to the stove, retrieved the plate, and set it in front of me. I jumped back quick as hell. She looked down at the plate and realized her mistake. She quickly grabbed it and threw the food in the garbage.

"Damn! I'm sorry. I forgot you were allergic to eggs. I'll fix you something else."

"Nah, ma, I'm good. But what's been up with you?"

"Work, work, and more work. I don't have much to do. I have no personal life outside of Saiyah and Macayla. I just wish Saiyah had told me what that bitch-ass nigga was doing to her. What type of best friend am I not to notice that my best friend was in trouble?" she said, breaking down crying.

I felt bad for Erian. Her and Saiyah had been best friends since before we met them, so I knew it was making her feel bad. "Erian, calm down. You ain't know, ma. Sometimes people are good at hiding their pain, and that's what she did. She hid it, bae. You know she wouldn't do shit to hurt you," I said, pulling her chin up to look at me.

I knew what I was about to do was wrong, but it felt right. Leaning down, I kissed her. She pushed me away instantly, before she pulled me back to her, wrapped her arms around my neck, and pulled me into a kiss.

Chapter 13

Erian

Pulling myself deeper into the kiss, I knew I should've pulled back, but the feeling in the pit of my stomach was so overwhelming that I couldn't stop. I felt his hands roaming down my backside, but I was caught up in the heat of the moment. De'Marrion was like a forbidden fruit that I knew I shouldn't be sampling, but I couldn't resist it.

As I felt myself being lifted off the ground, I wrapped my legs around his waist, while the tingling sensation between my legs increased. I was so lost in Mario and the kiss that I didn't realize he had pulled away.

"I missed you. I fucked up when I let you go. I regret even doing it. Forgive me, man."

"You were forgiven the moment you did it. I understood why you did what you did. I created doubt in us. I knew you would never cheat on me, and you loved me enough. I shouldn't have hit you that night, and I knew it took everything in you to hit me back. And I'm sorry for even taking you there."

"Nah, nah! No matter what you did, I should've never hit you back. A man should never hit a woman."

"And a woman should never hit a man unless she's ready for the consequences. I've been so sad on the inside since that incident. I wanted to reach out to you, but I figured you were better off without me."

"I just didn't want to feel like I was holding you back. You and Saiyah had academic scholarships to the colleges of y'all choices, and I was working a dead-end nine-to-five and other shit. So how you felt was how I felt ten times more. I loved you, Erian, even when I was with Chelley. My heart didn't beat the same with her. My chest didn't feel the same with her, and my love didn't reach the magnitude of when I was with you. I was in *like* with her, but you, ma, I was in love with you."

"I love you too, De'Marrion," I told him, placing a kiss on his lips.

"What you got planned for the rest of the day?" he asked me as his phone rang. He grabbed it, looked at it, then silenced it.

"Well, I have nowhere to go right now. My mom is upset, and I don't want to be around her, especially since Drew is still there, so Maceo offered to let me stay here in your room."

He nodded his head. "You going to be here when I get back?"

I nodded my head.

"Alright, Maceo and I got an emergency. Talk to Saiyah, bae. She already feels bad. Maceo told me as we sat in the cell how scared she was. Mace was released earlier than I was for different reasons, but we had time to talk. We all love Saiyah and know she has no one but you, and us now. Go talk to her." He gave me a kiss just as Maceo descended the stairs. He placed me on the ground and turned around.

"Aye, we gotta make this run right now," Maceo said.

Mario turned and nodded his head, and Maceo left out the door.

"Y'all go shopping and get something nice. When I get back, we're going on a date. Oh, and you need to put yo' two weeks in. Christina is planning to fire you and Saiyah.

Before she can do that, do that bitch dirty, especially since Travis too stuck on young pussy that's been around the block more than the mailman."

I burst out laughing at his last statement. I knew that bitch was going to try to fire me, but I wasn't too fucked up about her. I had been looking for new employment.

"Well, with no savings and no income, what am I supposed to do?"

"Go yo' ass back to school. I'll pay for it."

I shook my head.

His phone vibrated. "We can talk about it when I get back. Go check on Yah and do what I said," he told me.

"Go before Maceo keep calling you."

He bopped his head before walking out the door.

I went up to the room to check on Saiyah and Macayla. They were laid across the bed, sleeping. I eased the door closed and headed into the room to get some rest for a couple of hours. He wouldn't be back anytime soon.

Waking up refreshed, I threw on a Pink outfit and was out the door. I needed to get the outfit for that night. I didn't know where we were going, but I wanted to look nice. I drove to the mall and searched for A'Kira. After locating it, I went inside, and I instantly fell in love with the first dress I saw. The ruffles that flared out to the side made me fall in love with it. I decided that if we were going to a classy restaurant, I would wear this. Locating my size, I threw it across my arm and searched for three other outfits.

After spending another two and a half hours in that store and spending eight hundred dollars, I headed home to get ready. I was excited about our date, but it was short-lived when my phone rang.

"Hi, babe, how are you?" I asked Roman.

Now, I know I told Mario that I was single, and that was true. What Roman and I had wasn't your traditional boyfriend/girlfriend situation. He could have sex with other women, but I wasn't allowed to be in any sort of relations with a man. I didn't have a problem with it at first, but after a while, I wanted him for myself, and he refused, so I made it so that he could see me when I wanted to. I had love for Roman, but nothing compared to the love I had for myself and Mario. Mario would always hold the key to my heart.

"Nothing. Just getting back in. You busy? I'll come and grab you so we can do something. I miss you."

I rolled my eyes to the top of my head, praying they didn't get stuck. "Actually, I have other business to tend to. If you wanted me to make you a priority, you should've done the same."

"Why do you always end up doing this? It seems like every time I come back, you have a fucking problem with what I'm doing," he said with a heavy sigh, but I didn't care.

"I don't have a problem with it anymore. I could care less. You'll miss me more when I'm gone. I have business to tend to with Saiyah."

"Oh, yeah! I saw what you sent me, and I understand wanting to be there for your girl. Is she alright?"

"She's perfectly fine. I must go, Roman. I'll call you later."

"I love you, Erian."

"Mm-hmm, love you too," I said, before hanging up. That mothafucka didn't love anybody. I would fake it until I could make it. I prayed that Mario didn't find out about him because all hell would break loose.

Getting out of the car, I grabbed my bags and stumbled into the house. Saiyah came out of the kitchen and looked at me before coming over to help.

"What the hell? Erian, how much money did you spend in this damn store?"

"Close to eight hundred, but he got it. That black card lets me know he got it," I said, giggling.

"Oh, Lord. And then he gave you the card from hell. Maceo gave me his card, too, and told me to order my car online. We can pick it up when it's ready," she said.

I looked at my best friend and sister. She looked tired and exhausted. I don't know how I didn't notice it at first. "Yah, why didn't you come tell me?"

She looked at me for a moment before looking down at the counter. "I was embarrassed and ashamed. I allowed myself to be vulnerable and get raped. He would've never raped me had I put clothes on before I left the bathroom. Instead, I walked in a towel."

I just stared at Saiyah because this wasn't my best friend standing before me. "Yah, what are you saying? What are you talking about? Is that what that muthafucka told you?"

She nodded her head and wouldn't even look me in the face. Going around the counter, I pulled her chin up so we were face-to-face.

"Well, let me tell you one mothafucking thing. Fuck Drew! Drew gon' get his. Believe that, sis. Don't you ever in your life let me see you accept what a nigga like Drew says. He a pussy. To even threaten you and my g-baby is fucked up. You should've told me, Yah, and that nigga could've been dealt with. As your best friend, your sister, Macayla's godmother, it's my job to help you when you need me. If you ever in trouble again, promise me that you'll come talk to me." I pulled her into a hug.

"I promise I'll come to you. I was just trying to protect my baby. The first time he did it was after my six-week check-up. He claimed that he noticed me parading around in my towel while Macayla slept in her crib. Everyone was gone, and I didn't have anyone to go to. After he raped me twice, he told me I better not tell anyone, or he would kill my baby and make it look like an accident," she told me, bringing me to tears.

I couldn't believe this was the type of monster I was living with. I couldn't believe that Drew did her like that. I felt so bad for her because I could see that for the past six years, he had torn her down. I wished she would've told me years ago.

"I don't know what to do," she cried out.

Instead of giving my advice, I walked us to the couch and let her cry herself to sleep. By the time she had finally fallen asleep, I noticed that nighttime had arrived, and Macayla was also still asleep. Li'l Mace's grandfather had come to pick him up.

Getting up to get ready for my date, I texted Mario to see where we were going, but his phone was either dead or out of range because it kept showing up green in my iMessages. Instead of texting him, I called him, and it confirmed what I already knew. His phone was dead.

Since I didn't know where we were going, I just decided I would cook and let him eat when he got in the house. No need to spend money when his woman could cook, and I had gone shopping earlier, so it wasn't going to take long for my dinner to be done.

Chapter 14

Mario

Sitting in this small-ass room waiting for the meeting to start, I was growing irritated by the way shit was being run. Niggas was sitting around, gossiping about the head nigga in charge, and a lot of the shit they were saying sounded like they were overworked and underpaid. Shit, when I was a d-boy, I was making my extra shit by selling it through the drive-thru at Wendy's. Niggas knew where I would be at if they wanted to get served, but if yo' ass had change, then you had me fucked up because I wasn't serving you.

Watching my surroundings, I saw two clowns walk in. I wanted to laugh, but Maceo shook his head to silence me. I already knew who the niggas were, but I got a vibe from them I didn't like. Looking at Maceo, I saw he was feeling the same way.

The niggas stood in front of us. I guess they was waiting for mothafuckas to be quiet. When they saw that standing there wasn't getting them anywhere, they got shit in order, and I could tell I wasn't going to like what came out of their mouths.

"Jake and Freud ain't with us no mo'. Somebody killed them niggas, and I want to know who was behind it. It seems every time I turn around, mothafuckas is slipping."

Around the room, you could hear mumbling coming from the niggas who worked for us. Maceo and I just peeped the game that was coming from niggas, but two niggas stood out to me, and that was the two standing off to the side while the meeting was going on.

"I want eyes and ears to the street. Y'all have seventy-two hours to find out who the fuck killed them. Understood?"

There was a round of head nods.

"Another issue has come up. There seems to be some snakes in the camp. Money is being shorted, and product is missing, and ain't shit adding up. We'll be moving houses and letting y'all know the day-of what's going on. So, until further notice, close shop," the li'l nigga in charge said.

"I ain't trying to step on no toes or no shit like that, but um, I got a family to feed, and I can't afford to be out with no butter to put on my bread. Y'all got a timeline for how long shop gon' be closed?" I spoke up and asked.

"Honestly, I ain't gotta tell you a fucking thing. I said shop is closed, and I'll let y'all know when they back up and running. If you got an issue with that, then I don't know what to tell you."

I nodded my head because I saw the li'l nigga didn't know who I was. He was the new nigga that I had the distro put in place, but since this nigga didn't know how to talk, I would show him how.

"Y'all dismissed," he snapped.

I looked at Maceo, and I could see that nigga getting pissed by the second. We sat there until everybody was gone. They talked for a few minutes before they noticed us.

"What y'all still doing here? Is there an issue?" he asked, reaching for his gun.

Maceo stood up and looked at him. "I'm Murder, and this my brother, Trouble," Maceo stated. The two dudes looked back and forth between each other.

"So, what the fuck that's supposed to mean to us?"

I chuckled because that li'l nigga was trembling. He had to be five-ten, maybe 135 pounds with the Timbs on his feet, while my brother stood at six-three and 180 pounds.

"Shit, it doesn't have to mean shit to you. But how about I call up Booker and let him know that you talking to your workers like they ain't shit? And I'm sure Booker would be disappointed to hear that."

"Man, yo' threats don't mean shit to me," he snapped back.

"Trouble, call Booker."

"No need to. Freak, I see you haven't met Trouble and Murder Reed," Booker said from the speaker on my phone.

"What the fuck can those niggas do to me, Book? Not a mothafucking thing."

"I don't know. Why don't you ask them? They are standing before you."

His eyes grew big as hell as he looked between Maceo and me. I knew I was going to have to kill those niggas. His friend was just a liability, but he was going to have to die, too.

"Wha . . . aat are you talking about, Book?"

"De'Maceo and De'Marrion Reed, meet Frankie 'Freak' Robeson." The call ended.

"What? Y'all the Reeds? Why ain't nobody ever seen y'all niggas then?"

"Real Gs move in silence. Besides, no face, no case."

The young nigga relaxed a li'l, but I could see he was still stoic.

"I'ma be one hunnid with you. I don't want you running my team on this side at all. With all our workers, we show them respect. Just like we risk our lives every day, so do my li'l niggas. Respect is earned, not given, and if you didn't notice by now, none of them respect you. The people who killed dude was sitting right in your face. You don't have no order with yo' people, which is another reason I don't want you running my team," Maceo stated.

"I put this whole team together by myself. Y'all niggas can't make me step down from no position that I earned."

I looked at Maceo and saw the ticking in his jaw, letting me know that he was getting irritated.

"You got two options. Step down, or get dropped down."

"What the fuck you mean, dropped down?"

"Let's just say your mother's new favorite color is going to be black."

"Y'all threatening me?" he asked. The look on his face let me know that he didn't think we were.

"Mario, talk to this muthafucka, because he is pissing me off."

I didn't want to do any talking. Removing my gun from my back, I put two in that nigga's head, then turned to his partner. His hands were already up in fear. When I talked to Booker, I was cussing that nigga out. These niggas were pussies. I shot him in the head, and his body dropped to the floor. Going over to them, I saw both were dead and not moving.

Grabbing my phone, I placed a call back to Booker. "Booker, I need my house cleaned."

"Damn, again? Yo' ass don't need to be having no parties."

"Shut yo' ass up, nigga. Make sure my house clean. You know what I mean," Maceo said and ended the call.

"Have Troop find out who those other two niggas are, and I'll find new locations for the houses. I gotta find the girls a place to stay. Saiyah don't even look comfortable with me," he said, and I could tell that he was in his feelings about it.

"Bro, give it a minute. She just made some tough confessions. She needs some time alone. Let her have it, and you get to know your daughter."

"Can you believe that shit? Macayla almost six, and Li'l Maceo is three. I got two kids, and yo' ass still ain't got none."

I thought about what he said, and a sadness came over me. I would've been had my first son by now, but Erian lost him when she was five and a half months. His umbilical cord wrapped around his neck. I walked around with the picture of him in my wallet. Maceo and Saiyah didn't even know about him, and I was sure Erian didn't want them to know.

"I'll have some one day. If I can get shit together, maybe I can get Erian back."

"Sis want you back. I just hope you done with that bitch, Chelley. Where you find her green ass at, again? She one bitch you had that I hated."

"Yo, she thought I wasn't going to find out she was cheating on me. I've been done with the bitch. No lie, my dick is drier than a desert fucking with her. I ain't even slid in another shorty. The closest I got to a female was with Erian."

"Damn! Nigga, not you. You were hoeing like I don't know what when you and Erian broke up," he said, laughing.

I mugged his ass because he had me fucked up. "I'm tired of that shit. I just wanna lay up under one bitch, and that's the bitch I wanna marry, but I can't see shit past Erian."

"I know what you saying, bro."

For the remainder of the ride home, I just sat back in the seat and thought about all the bullshit I had been through, from a crackhead as a mama to an invisible-ass daddy. I didn't give two fucks about the past, only my present and future, and I prayed that Erian and I could fix this shit.

As we pulled into Maceo's driveway, I saw the cars still in the same place. Getting out and walking to the door, I keyed in the door code and pushed the door open. The entire house was completely quiet. Walking up the stairs to my bedroom, I saw Erian lying across it in a t-shirt and a scarf on her head. Looking at the clock, I saw that it was after eleven, and I was tired as shit. I didn't even realize all that fucking time had passed. After we had left that spot, I went to see Booker so I could get in that nigga ass for those bitch-ass niggas who was running our shit.

Stripping out my clothes, I got in the bed and pulled her to me. Her eyes opened, and she looked up at me.

"What time is it?" she asked, and I covered my nose as I laughed at her.

"Shit, time for you to brush yo' teeth."

She hit me, and I laughed at her again.

"Nah, ma, but it's after eleven. I didn't even realize we was gone so long. I apologize for being late. Reschedule the date for a later date? Did you even go to the mall?"

"Yeah, my clothes are in your drawers. I cooked you some food, and it's down in the oven. Did you want it?"

"Hell, yeah! What you cook?"

"I grilled some sirloin steaks with stuffed bell peppers and a baked potato with butter and sour cream like you like it."

"Girl, get yo' ass up and go get my food," I said, smacking her on the ass.

"Stop, Mario. What do you want to drink?" she asked me, slipping some pants on.

"Shit, Maceo ass got some Pepsi. Grab me two of 'em," I told her as I lay back in the bed.

She left the room to go get my food. I grabbed the remote, turned the TV on, and watched the ID channel. The door opened about fifteen minutes later, and she brought my food in on a tray. Sitting up, I grabbed it from her, then patted the side of the bed. After she sat down, I didn't waste any time devouring the food. It was good as fuck. Reminded me of us back in the day when she would cook for me.

"Mario, you better slow down before yo' ass choke," she said, staring at me while I was eating.

"I'm hungry as fuck. Chelley ass couldn't cook to save her fucking life. Last four years, my ass been eating takeout. And the one time she tried to cook, I ended up with food poisoning. I promised myself that I would never eat that shit again," I told her, still putting the food in my mouth.

"How old is she? She better be a young-ass girl."

I swallowed my food before answering her question. "Man, hell nah. Chelley is older than you and me. She is fucking thirty-two."

"Mario, you were fucking with some old pussy," she said, bursting out laughing and leaning on me.

I looked at her ass with a mug on my face. "Man, get the fuck off me," I snapped at her.

She was still laughing, but when she looked up in my face, her ass burst out laughing again. I drank the rest of my pop and set the tray on the nightstand before turning around and kicking her ass out of my bed. She flew on the floor, and I lay back in the bed with my arms behind my head.

A few seconds had passed, so I looked over to see her ass wasn't on the floor. I reclined back into the bed, and her ass jumped on me, scaring the fuck outta me. I pushed her ass off me so quick, and she started laughing at me as she lay at the foot of the bed.

"You should've seen yo' face, man. Ol' scary ass. You still think about that cat, don't you?"

"Fuck you, Erian." Her ass knew I hated fucking cats ever since that cat attacked me when I was a kid. I be avoiding them mothafuckas. If a bitch had a cat, she had to put that li'l mothafucka up before I slid through.

"I know you want to, but you can't," she said, bending over, twerking.

I watched that ass bounce up and down. My dick was getting hard as she dropped to the floor and kept twerking.

"Get your hot ass up! Get in the bed, man," I said, laughing at her as I readjusted myself.

"Don't get mad because yo' dick hard as fuck." She climbed on the bed and sat on my lap. "You mad, daddy. I'm sorry. I'll make it up to you," she said, rocking back and forth on my lap.

I closed my eyes, and a low growl left my lips as she continued doing what she was doing. I wanted to fuck her li'l ass, but I wanted to start our shit off the right way, and this wasn't the way.

Grabbing her hips, I looked up at her as she looked down at me. I slid her off my lap and went to the bathroom. Closing the door, I turned the shower on cold and got in. It was going to be a long night.

Chapter 15

Maceo

Standing at the doorway, I watched Saiyah and Macayla as they cuddled up to each other in the bed. I wished shit was different and I could be there with them, but knowing what Yah Yah had been through had me pulling back from her. It wasn't my intention to pull back from her, but I could see that she wasn't feeling me, so I was going to let her rock for the moment.

Closing the bedroom door, I headed down into the studio to get this beat right for True. True was my li'l homie from around the way, an upcoming Chicago rapper. He had bars and lyrics for days, but I needed that nigga to get that one single that would take him to the top. Starting up my laptop, I threw on my Beats by Dre and listened to the lyrics he had sent me to make a beat, too. After the laptop was powered up, I went into the file for True and listened to it. I knew what I needed to do. Tweaking it for a minute, I finally got the sound that I needed.

After sending it out to True, I started writing music for this new rapper named Guam. Now, his ass couldn't rap for shit, but the nigga had money. I could write the nigga a hot-ass song, but I couldn't get that nigga to rap.

Twenty minutes or so passed before I heard the basement door open. Turning toward the door, I saw Saiyah with Macayla in her arms. Getting up, I grabbed Macayla from her, and she wrapped her arms around my neck.

Reaching my hand out, I grabbed Saiyah's hand. "What's up? Why y'all down here and not in the bed?"

"Well, I told Macayla about who you were, and she wanted to meet you officially."

I looked down at baby girl. She looked just like her mama with the black, curly hair and dimples in her cheeks.

"What's up, baby girl?"

"Hi, Daddyyy," she said nervously.

I smiled at her because she acted just like Saiyah ass. "Yo' mama said that you wanted to meet me and talk to me. So what you want to know?"

"What's your name? Mommy said it's Maceo."

"De'Maceo Santana Reed-Perkins. What's your name?"

"Macayla Santaria Perkins. I'm five and a half. How old are you?"

"I'll be twenty-nine in two weeks."

For the rest of the night, we got to know each other until she fell asleep in my arms. Most nights, I fell asleep in the studio, so I had a bed down there. Getting up, I laid her in the bed and went to sit back down.

Saiyah was writing in the notebook where I had my lyrics.

"What you writing, Yah?"

She slid the notebook over to me, and I read it. The song was dope as fuck. I didn't know that she could even write. If she was up for it, she could be writing hits for people, and I could make it happen

"Damn! This you? Why you ain't tell me that you could write? All them years I knew you and never knew you could write."

"Nobody ever asked, and I had to do something to stay sane in that house. I love my parents, but I'm better off without them."

I nodded my head, but I wanted to know about dude. I knew that she wasn't going to tell anybody, so I was going to ask. "Yah, why you ain't tell nobody about dude?"

She looked at me before exhaling. "I was thinking about Macayla. I didn't enjoy the shit that Drew was doing, but if it kept my baby safe, then I was for it. We had always been close, but I never thought he would do anything like that to me. It had been going on for years, and I was embarrassed to tell Ms. Erin. I didn't want her to think I was some sort of hoe. If I could go back in time, I would've told her the first time, especially after he said I wanted him."

I nodded my head and understood why she ain't say anything. "Let me ask you something, though?"

"What's up?"

"It's early, and I know I fucked up in the past, but can you please help me help you," I said, rolling over to her in the chair and grabbing her hand.

"Maceo, I don't know. I've been through so much since you walked outta my life all those years ago. I'm not the same person that I used to be."

"You look like the same person, Yah. If I help you, can you get back to her? I love you, Saiyah. I just want what I had back then. No woman has ever compared to you, and I can't keep looking for her, nor waiting when I know my heart wants you. You're all I need, you and my kids."

"Yeah, about Tee. Maceo, please don't make me beat that girl ass. She's going to keep testing my soul, and I'm not beat for her, baby."

"Man, fuck Tee, straight like that. I regret even fucking with that bird-brain-ass bitch. I fucked her three times, and I got Li'l Mace outta that."

"I see you got you a junior."

"Li'l Mace ain't no junior. His name is T'Maceo. She be lying, telling people that he a junior. She didn't even know my name. I've been dealing with her shit for too long. Now she pregnant again, claiming that baby is mine. We smashed a couple months ago when I was lit, but I don't believe that shit. Tee is a scheming, scamming-ass bitch, and I wouldn't dare drop my dick off in her hot-ass pussy again. The times that I hit it, her pussy was looser than water running through your fingers. I provided her with a decent life off the strength of my son, then her stupid ass turns around and catches a drug case that could send her ass up the creek. I'm not beat for Tee. I want you, Saiyah."

She looked at me for a minute, debating before she agreed. I got up and pulled her into a hug.

"But I have some conditions. One, I want you to still get us our apartment for now. I've been living with people for as long as I can remember. I want some alone time. Secondly, you can get Macayla on the weekends. Last but not least, don't bring up this conversation about dude or what happened. I'm okay. I'm not scarred for life. I'm going to still want to twerk and have sex. He could never take away who I am and what I want to be. He didn't even put a dent into my life. I believe he thinks he destroyed me, but he's made me stronger, and I won't stop until I get back on top. I'm going to enroll in school and get my degree. I don't have a lot of money saved up, but I have enough to pay you for the apartment and car."

"Monday, when you get off work," I told her, but I wanted to acknowledge what she said. "I know you not the same Saiyah I met at seventeen and was willing to do whatever to keep a nigga, but you also have not nor never will be weak. I accept your glow up, ma, but please believe me, you ain't going to be in that apartment alone because a nigga will be sliding through to see you. Trust and believe that," I said, leaning us back against the sound board.

"You love me, Saiyah?" I asked.

"You know I'ma always love you, Maceo."

"Give me a kiss then," I told her.

She leaned down and looked at me before kissing me on the cheek. I nodded my head at her because I knew she wasn't ready, and this proved it. I was going to fall back until she came to me.

"I'ma get her up to bed. Will you show me my apartment tomorrow?"

I nodded my head as I let her out of my embrace. She stood up, went to Macayla, and picked her up before heading toward the door.

I sat back down as she walked out of the room, then I picked up my phone and looked through my messages. I saw that Malika had sent me a message about twenty minutes ago. It was an image of her in the living room with nothing on.

I should've turned her down, but I couldn't. Saiyah wasn't going to be ready anytime soon, so for the moment, I was going to keep fucking with Malika. Instead of texting her back, I called her.

"Hey, zaddy!" she purred into the phone.

"What's up? I see you just sent me something about twenty minutes ago. You still want me to slide through?"

"Of course I do. I wouldn't have hit you up if I wasn't waiting on you. I just got off and could use some dick right now."

"Say less! I'm on my way."

Getting up, I walked out the door. Saiyah was standing there with her arms folded. She caught me off guard since Macayla wasn't with her. The look on her face told me that she had heard the entire conversation. Before I could even say anything, she turned around and ran up the stairs.

Fuck! I thought as I ran up behind her. Catching the end of her shirt, I pulled her down the stairs, placing my hand over her mouth to prevent her from waking up the whole house. She was fighting for me to let her go, but I grabbed her tighter and took her into the other room and closed the door with my foot.

As I placed her on the bed, she looked up at me, then kicked me in the leg. Dragging her ass to the edge of the bed, I pulled her face close to mine.

"What the issue, Yah?"

"So, you were really going to fuck another bitch. Really, Maceo? Why ask me about a relationship when you're not ready?"

"First off, I didn't ask about a relationship. I asked you about getting back to who you used to be. I can see in your eyes that you are not ready, and you won't be for a while."

"All you want is pussy? I'll give it to you, if that's what you want," she said, proceeding to take off her clothes. I tried to stop her, but she kept going.

"Yah! Stop! Stop, Saiyah, damn."

"Why are you doing this, Maceo? Like, why are you willing to leave me again? Like you couldn't wait until I went upstairs to call some other hoe. Like that's where we at?" She was crying, damn near hysterical.

"Saiyah, calm down, bae. I didn't think you was ready for all of that. I thought you weren't ready for a relationship nor ready to even go further. You need to fix it, Yah. You're not ready for us."

"I'm ready. I'm ready now, Maceo. I promise that I am. Look, I'll give you whatever you want."

I shook my head because that's not what I wanted from her. I wanted her to be back to Saiyah, the one who smiled at simple shit and loved the corny shit I used to say. I wanted the Saiyah whose virginity I took. The

Saiyah who loved me when I was struggling. The Saiyah who wiped blood off my face when I got into that fight. I want the Saiyah Brady that I fell in love with.

"Saiyah, I don't want that shit. It won't work like that. You gotta find your way back to me on your own, not because you hear I'm about to go fuck another bitch. Fall back in love with me because that's what you want, and that's what I'm showing you, baby. Fucking ol' girl don't mean shit. Just a quick way to get a nut off. I don't love that bitch. I love you, but you ain't the same, Saiyah. I can't feel yo' vibe. I used to be able to feel yo' vibe, connect with yo' spirit and soul. I can't even feel that, Saiyah. It's almost like you aren't there," I said, looking at her as she cried.

"Maceo, why are you doing this? I am the same person that I used to be. Why can't you see that?"

"Alright, Yah. If you say you the same, you wouldn't be doing this right here. You not the same. I can feel that shit in my heart. You not the girl I fell in love with."

She dropped her head and looked at me. "So, you don't love me, Maceo?"

"Saiyah, do you hear yourself? I don't love you? If I didn't, I wouldn't have done the shit I did the other day. Or I wouldn't be right here talking to you. I could've left and fucked ol' girl, but instead, I'm standing here while she is blowing me up. If I didn't love you, I would've been knee deep in some pussy, but I'm not. I'm trying to get you to see that I love you, Saiyah, but before we can go anywhere, you need to get back to Saiyah. The woman sitting before me is broken and vulnerable. I ain't never seen you so weak before. You're begging me to fuck you. You're begging me not to leave you. This not you, ma. Go upstairs and go to sleep. I'll sleep in the guest room, next to you and Macayla," I stated.

She got up and rushed up the stairs. I blew out a breath of frustration. My phone rang for the tenth time, and I was getting irritated.

"Why are you blowing up my fucking phone like this, yo?"

"Nigga, what's with the fucking attitude? I've been waiting for you. Where the fuck you at?"

"At home with my girl. Real shit, lose my number," I snarled at her before hanging up and blocking her. I had other shit to worry about than her dick-thirsty ass.

Dragging myself up the stairs to the guest bedroom, I stopped to check on Saiyah. Entering the room, I could hear her sniffling, and baby girl was lying on her side, wiping Saiyah's tears as her own cascaded down her cheeks. That shit broke my heart because in a matter of twenty-four hours, I saw how much Saiyah loved our daughter. They were thick as thieves.

I tapped Saiyah. She looked up at me, then down at Macayla.

"Scoot over, Yah."

She scooted over, and I got in the bed with them. Macayla looked as if she was going to sleep.

"Why you crying, Yah? Then you got Macayla crying, too? What's up with you for real?" She gave me the cold shoulder, and I let her have her moment. After about thirty minutes, I realized that she had fallen asleep. Instead of getting up, I laid next to them and went to sleep myself.

Chapter 16

Saiyah

After the exhausting night I had with Maceo, I couldn't have agreed more with what he was saying. I couldn't feel Maceo's vibe, and if I couldn't feel his, then I knew he couldn't feel mine. I wish I could go back to the old Saiyah, but I didn't know how. With everything that happened over the last couple of years, I had built a wall around my heart. Everybody I loved had either left me or let me down. The only people who didn't turn their backs on me were Erian and her mother, Erin. I loved them to death, but I didn't know if Ms. Erin would ever look at me the same again. She had put on a strong act in that house that night, but then she bailed Drew outta jail, and he was living with her. She hadn't called me, nor Erian, but I figured that she wouldn't want to talk to me. I loved her to death, but not enough to still want to be in the presence of the man who had me living in fear.

Sitting up in the bed, I kept looking between Maceo and Macayla. I knew that I needed to get some help. I didn't want to lose them both.

As I tried to ease out the bed, Maceo grabbed me.

"We gotta get you some help, baby mama. I haven't cried since the day I found out you got the abortion, but last night, I shed a few tears with you and my baby. You not the same, Yah."

I didn't want to keep crying, so I nodded my head.

"Talk, Yah, and tell me what's going on."

"I've lost so much over the years, and I'm afraid I'm going to lose you, too. Life hasn't been fair to me, but I have no clue where I went wrong."

"You went wrong because you lost faith in not only God, but yourself. When you don't operate on faith, ma, you lose more than you anticipated."

I just nodded my head again.

"No faith, no power. Little faith, little power. Much faith, much power. All Faith, all power."

"I don't have faith in anything, Mace. I don't know why or when I lost it. Maybe it depleted over the years, but I don't know how to get it back."

"You just gotta believe change is going to come. I love you, Saiyah, but if we ain't connecting, then how we gon' work on a relationship? Yeah, I know last night was wrong of me, but I didn't honestly think you wanted to be with me. You stepped outta my embrace when I held you close. I know I hurt you, but you hurt me worse than I could ever hurt you."

"But Macayla is right here," I grunted out.

"Think back to that day, Yah. You weren't even going to tell me you were pregnant or getting an abortion."

I sat back against the headboard and thought about the day that I found out that I was pregnant. I wasn't going to tell him, but his ass found out through my emails that were connected to his phone.

"Saiyah! Mommy!" I heard Maceo and Macayla.

I looked at them and smiled. "What's up?"

"We want breakfast, Mommy. Daddy, you like pancakes? Titi Eri make good ones."

"Yeah, Mommy! Me and Macayla hungry." Maceo mimicked her.

"Alright! Alright. Get up, both of you, and go wash your face and brush your teeth so you can eat."

Maceo smiled as he picked Macayla up and they went into the bathroom. He came out of the bathroom a few seconds later and stood in front of me.

"This conversation isn't over, but I think you need to go back to the beginning. I apologize for my mistake, but you have yet to apologize for yours. A few years ago, I had to go to a therapist for some shit, but it helped. We going to see her first thing tomorrow. You need the help. Not just for me or you, but for our daughter. I'ma keep repeating that I love you because I do, but we not going anywhere until you talk to somebody."

"Okay, Maceo. Now get back in there with Macayla before she lies about brushing her teeth."

"A'ight." He pulled me into a hug. It lingered for a minute before he pulled back.

"Daddy, look!" Macayla called out to him. He walked into the bathroom and helped her with whatever she was calling him for, then left the room.

I was shocked by how relaxed Macayla was around him. Usually, she was guarded and didn't trust people, but with Maceo and Mario, she trusted them very quickly.

Walking in the bathroom, I washed my face and hands before heading into the kitchen. Everyone stopped talking when they saw me rounding the corner.

"Why y'all stop talking?"

"Saiyah, I don't want you to get upset, but my mother wants you to come grab your things from the house, and she said she would like a formal apology from you for disrespecting her house."

I laughed at the obvious joke, but I stopped when I saw that everyone wasn't laughing.

"Are you serious? What do I owe her an apology for? Her husband was raping me. I'm not apologizing for a damn thing." I turned around and headed out the door. I didn't have shoes on nor a coat, but I didn't give a fuck.

Walking down the streets, I was so pissed that she thought I was going to apologize to her. Oh, she had me fucked up. Apologize? Every time I heard that word, the shit blew me up.

I heard a car coming behind me. I didn't recognize it, so I kept walking. The person blew the horn, and I turned around again, and Maceo looked at me as he stood next to the car with his arms folded.

"You running? What was all that talk that you were spitting last night? All that you're stronger and not going to let it get you down. Looking at you now, I can see that it was all bullshit. Before you stormed out, Ms. Erin wanted you to apologize for putting Macayla in harm when you should've come to her."

I started to speak, but he walked up on me, hushing me. "Before you even open your mouth and say anything, just get in the car so we can go home, and I can take you to y'all new apartment," he said to me.

I wanted to argue back, but he turned his back and got in the car.

Getting in the car, I sat in silence as he drove. Maceo glanced at me every now and then, but I knew he was pissed. I just sat in the seat until we pulled into the driveway.

"You need to talk to Macayla. What you did in there was irrational, cussing in front of Macayla. She cried after you left. She doesn't understand why you mad at her, honey. I think you need to explain it, not none of us." With that, he got out of the car and went into the house.

I just sat there dumbfounded. How was I going to explain it to Macayla?

Chapter 17

Erian

"Did I say something wrong? Like, I know it sounded bad, but she didn't even let me finish. I'm not used to this Saiyah."

"I'm not going to lie to you, ma. Your wording was a little fucked up. I don't think you should've said it the way you did. It made it seem like your mother wanted an apology for Saiyah getting raped by your stepdaddy, so I see why she acted like she did, but she's going through some changes. Maceo just told us that he thinks she needs professional help."

"Oh, okay. I understand. I guess I should've worded it differently, but I didn't think she would react like that."

Mario just stared at me before peering back at the door and Macayla in the living room.

"Saiyah needs help. You can't help her, and neither can anybody else until she sees a professional. Maceo is going to move her and Macayla into their own apartment today and give her one of his whips until hers come in. You, on the other hand, will be coming with me. And before you protest, you'll be in the apartment building next to Saiyah."

"Mario, I have to tell you something," I told him nervously. I didn't know how he was going to take me having a boyfriend, but Roman was always away on business and bitches, and we hadn't spoken since yesterday.

"What's up?"

"Uh, I have a boyfriend."

He dropped my hands quickly and looked at me. For a second, he stared at me before turning around and walking out the door. I waited for him to return, but after ten minutes and no sign of him, I gave up. I sighed with defeat and went into the living room with Macayla as I waited for the breakfast pizza she wanted.

Thirty minutes later, the timer went off, and I retrieved the pizza from the oven just as the front door opened. Turning around, I saw Mario, Maceo, and Saiyah walking toward me. Setting the pizza on the counter and checking it, I knew Macayla was going to be happy. It had sausage, eggs, bacon, potatoes, cheese, and biscuits. I knew Mario couldn't eat it, so I made him a breakfast shake and made him toast with bacon.

Fixing everybody's plate and calling Macayla into the kitchen, I grabbed Mario's epi-pen and set it next to him just in case, then proceeded to eat my food. The table was eerily quiet, and I didn't know what to do, so I kept eating my food until Maceo broke the silence.

"Macayla, how would you like to live with Daddy while Mommy goes on a vacation?"

"Really? Mommy, I can stay with Daddy!"

Saiyah looked at Maceo, and he just stared back at her.

"Sure, baby. Daddy said you can decorate your own room how you want it, and he'll buy you whatever you want," Saiyah said mischievously.

Maceo smiled at her, obviously aware of what she was doing.

"Yay! Titi Erian, I get to stay with my daddy."

"I see, Pooh. Your daddy is going to spoil you rotten."

"Sure am, princess. Matter of fact, how about you go get washed up so I can take you shopping right now? Mommy is going on vacation tomorrow, so let's go get her a gift."

Saiyah rolled her eyes as Macayla hopped up and ran up the stairs. As soon as she was out of earshot, Saiyah snapped on Maceo. I had never seen her in the rare form that she was in now.

"What the fuck do you think you're doing, Maceo? You trying to turn my baby against me by buying her shit? Is that what you're doing now? Who the fuck does you think you are? I carried her for nine months and three days. I was in labor for thirty-six hours, and I'm the one who pushed her out. You weren't even fucking there, and this is how you choosing to do me. For real?"

Maceo kept eating his food, unfazed, and I just stared at Saiyah like she was crazy. Ever since Drew said what he said two days ago, it was like some switch in her flipped, and it flipped quickly.

"Saiyah, can I, uh, talk to you on the deck, please?" I said to her.

She looked at me before getting up and storming out to the deck. I looked at Maceo, and he shook his head, but I could see in his eyes that he was concerned about Saiyah and didn't know what to do.

"Give it some time, Maceo. Please don't give up on her. I know she really loves you."

"I don't know this Saiyah, and until the Saiyah I know returns, I don't have much to say. She been acting real irrational and not caring what she does or how she reacts in front of Macayla. Saiyah's issues are deeper than me, and I can't help her. She needs professional help, and tomorrow, she's going to turn herself in, no questions asked. Either she gets help, or I'll file for emergency custody of my daughter."

I looked to see if Maceo was serious, and he was. I got up and walked to the deck with Saiyah. "Saiyah, what's going on with you?" I asked, closing the sliding doors.

"Maceo is what's wrong with me. Do you know after he talked to me 'bout getting back to myself, he was about to leave to fuck another bitch?"

I looked at her, confused as to why she was mad. "Okay, and? You're not his woman, and I'm not saying that to be on his side. But you've been out of his life for a while, and you're acting the opposite of who he used to know. You were much more mature at seventeen and eighteen. Maceo was twenty-one, fucking around with you, so I see why he assumed you've changed. What's your issue? Ever since Drew said that you wanted it, you've been acting weird."

I saw her go stiff, and she kept shifting her feet, and her shoulders dropped a little bit. She wasn't standing as tall as she once was.

"That is what it is, isn't it? Do you believe Maceo believes that?" I asked.

"He does believe it. I saw the way he looked at me, Erian, and he could've come to me to have sex, but instead, he was going to see another woman."

Now, I was almost certain that Saiyah was going crazy. "You were raped less than forty-eight hours ago, and you wanted that man to have sex with you. Sis, I don't understand what you're saying."

"I'm saying Maceo won't ever look at me the same anymore. He thinks I'm dirty and tainted. He was willing to go sleep with another woman after talking to me about our future. I know he doesn't want me in that way. I can feel it deep down that he doesn't want me."

Maceo came out onto the porch. "I ain't never said no shit like that, so don't be out here lying to Erian. I told you I couldn't feel yo' vibe. When I brought you in my arms, your breathing picked up, your heart was damn near jumping out of your chest, and you pulled back almost instantly. I can't even get you to kiss me, Yah.

What you talking about? What that nigga did don't make me blind to the fact that you're beautiful as hell, or that I still wanna marry yo' ass. You gotta find a way back to you, Yah. Look at how you had Macayla woke with you, crying. How you were cussing and carrying on earlier before you stormed out the house. You're being irrational, ma, and that ain't you.

"This rehab you going to is going to get you some help. Your issues started before Drew. So, I need you to either go to the rehab or hand over custody of Macayla for the time being. You'll be giving temporary guardianship to Erian. She known Macayla longer, and baby girl trust her." Maceo spoke his piece, then gave her time to come to her own conclusion.

Saiyah looked like she wanted to debate hard as hell with Maceo, but she knew better.

"I'll go to the rehab, but I want to talk to Macayla every morning and night. And I want to be included in decisions that you make for her. If I can't help, then Erian will hold judgment on my behalf. I don't want the courts involved. Is that agreeable?" she asked him.

He nodded his head and walked over to her, and she backed up. He backed up and threw his hands up in surrender. "Just like I thought, Yah. You ain't ready. Stop worrying about another bitch. Get you some help, and we'll be waiting on you." Maceo walked away, then turned around to say something, but opted not to do so before walking into the house.

I looked at Saiyah, but she turned her head. I didn't know what I could do to help my best friend turned sister, but I prayed this rehab could help her. I had never seen her this way, and it was tearing me up on the inside. I swiped the tears away as I walked into the house.

Macayla was coming down the stairs and running to Maceo. He picked her up and spun her around. She laughed and giggled. I watched in awe as the two laughed together. It seemed Maceo was a good dad, and I didn't think he'd need much help from me.

"Break up with yo' nigga," I heard behind me.

Mario was standing there staring at me. Instead of entertaining him, I walked away to my room. I could feel him behind me, but I didn't care. Walking into the room, I tried to close the door, but he pushed it open.

"So, you ain't gon' do it?" he asked.

"You're asking me to break up with my man, and for what?"

"You weren't thinking about yo' man when we were sixty-nining up in this bitch this morning. I wouldn't have even done the shit if I knew you belonged to another nigga."

"Whatever, Mario. You're making it a big deal."

"Erian, I don't think you understanding, so let me help you understand." He closed and locked the door. He walked over to me, and I had to look that nigga up and down. My five-five, 145-pound frame didn't have shit on his six-two, 185-pound frame.

He picked me up, and I wrapped my arms around his neck. His tongue traced the outline of my neck. Every spot he licked, he went back and kissed. I wanted to stop him, but the moisture and throbbing between my legs wasn't allowing me. Feeling us move, I opened my eyes and saw that he was about to lay me down on the bed.

"Take that shit off," he growled.

Hurriedly, I took my clothes off. In a weird way, I was turned on.

"Come on, ma. Ass up, face down," he said, and I turned over. He slapped his hands across my ass cheeks.

I looked over my shoulder and didn't see him, and soon, I realized why when I felt his tongue touch my clit.

Earlier, he took his time, but this time, he was showing no mercy.

“You going to leave that nigga?” he asked me in between slurps and licks.

“Yes! I’ll leave him,” I yelled out. De’Marrion Reed’s head game was official.

“Call that nigga right now,” he said, throwing my phone on the bed. Grabbing it, I dialed Roman’s number, and after a few rings, he answered.

“Hello, Erian. How are you today?”

“I can’t do this anymore. I’m breaking up with you,” I moaned into the phone.

“Wha—? What the hell are you doing?” he yelled into the phone.

“No . . . thing!” I yelled out as Mario sucked my little pebble into his mouth.

“Tell that nigga why,” he said, smacking me on the ass again, making me yelp.

“I can’t be with you because I’m not in love with you. The only man I love is . . . oh my God, Mario, right there,” I yelled out, as his fingers slid inside of me and he slurped all over my clit.

“Mario? Who the fuck is Mario? What the fuck are you doing, Erian?”

“I’m coming!” I screamed out.

Mario kept going, but I pushed his head back.

“Erian! Erian! What is going on?” I heard Roman yelling.

I fell on the bed, and Mario walked around and snatched the phone off the bed. Wiping his face with my shirt, he put the phone on speakerphone.

“Nigga, lose this fucking number. Whatever you and my girl had been over. If I find out you called or even contacted her in any way, I'll be at yo' mothafucking door. Fuck off my woman's line." Mario hung up the phone and threw it on the bed.

"You heard what I said. Same goes for you."

"You're petty."

"I don't give a fuck. Come ride this dick."

Chapter 18

Mario

Watching Erian strut over to me, I was engulfed in her beautiful, chocolate skin. Her hips were wider and more defined while her black, curly hair cascaded around her face. I licked my lips as she dropped down in front of me. She looked back up at me through her thick eyelashes. Her eyes went down as she looked at my hard dick that was in her hands. She was slowly moving her hand up and down, and I opened my eyes just as she took me in her mouth.

I could tell she hadn't done this in a long time, and the fact that I grew some more was making her gag. I could tell from her facial expression that she was getting frustrated.

"Erian, slow down, bae."

She nodded her head and started over again. After a few attempts, she was deep throating my shit, and my ass was damn near about to be screaming. Her jaws were sunken in as she continued doing what she was taught to do. She removed him from her mouth, making a popping noise before she drew him back in, and I noticed that this time was much sloppier than before. If I thought she completely forgot the shit I taught her, then I was lying. My baby had a nigga about to scream like a bitch, clenching my ass cheeks together, no homo, and my toes throwing up gang signs. She was putting in work, and the shit was nice and sloppy like I liked it. I felt my nut rising, so I pushed her back.

"I told you to come ride this dick."

"Unh-uh, where the condom at?"

I looked at her ass sideways. "Ain't you on birth control? I don't even have one. Bring yo' ass on, girl."

"No, Mario. We not having sex unless you have a condom."

"Erian, shut up and just ride this dick. I ain't been with nobody in months. Can you please just sit on it for a few seconds? If after that you still want it, I'll go get the condom from Maceo room if you want me to."

She looked hesitant, but she came over to me. Wrapping my arms around her waist, I picked her up and eased her down.

"Mmmmmm! Fuck!"

"Ride it like you own it."

She rocked back and forth for a few minutes, getting adjusted. Pulling one of her big-ass titties to my lips, I sucked on them chocolate drops she called nipples.

"Ssss, Mario."

Standing us up, I let her take control as I walked us over to the bed. Laying down, she took that as an opportunity to ride me with no hands. If her ass didn't slow down, I was going to be cumming soon.

"Erian, slow down." I grabbed her hips, trying to stop her, but she kept going.

Flipping her over and holding her in a tight hold, I gave her them deep, long strokes. Burying my face in the crook of her neck, I kissed her spots.

"Ohhhh, Mario. Right there." Her feet dug into my legs, pulling me closer into her.

"Give me a kiss, Erian."

She gave me a kiss and tightened her muscles around me. I pulled outta her before I could nut.

"Ass up! Face down. You already know daddy want that arch on point."

She looked at me, flipped over, and I had to admire that arch she had in her back. Pulling her to the edge of the bed, I slammed into her.

"Maaa . . . rio," she yelled out as I deep-stroked that pussy.

I could feel her pussy pulsating around my dick, so I continued to stroke until I saw that thick cream cover it. Grabbing her ponytail, I pulled her up as I continued to stroke her sugary walls.

"Damn, you know this my pussy right, Erian? If I find out another nigga touched what's mine, I'm killing him and you." When I said that, my pussy got wetter. Yeah, you read it right. *My* pussy got wetter. It was mine.

"Baby, I'm cumming," she yelled out as I continued to slam into her.

"Fawwkkkk! Me, too," I growled out as I let my nut shoot all up in her.

Pulling out of her, I rolled to the side of her. "Damn, you still got that trap-me pussy."

"Fuck you, Mario," she huffed and puffed out.

I laughed at her ass. I looked back over at her, and her ass was falling asleep. I smacked her on the ass, and she yelped then mugged me.

"Go get yo' ass in the shower so I can take you to the apartment then furniture shopping."

She mumbled under her breath as she walked into the bathroom, but I wasn't thinking about her smart-mouth ass. Hearing the shower water running, I hopped up and went to join her. I knew what I was in for with Erian.

I just hoped we never got back to the place where we wouldn't be speaking again.

The next day . . .

Pulling up to the rehab, I turned to look at Erian. She was already crying, and I couldn't deal with that shit. Saiyah was in the front seat with an attitude and didn't want anybody speaking to her. Maceo didn't care about her attitude, but it seemed Erian was surprised by it.

"Saiyah, you wanna say bye to your best friend? You know, the girl who is like your sister and been rocking with you for I don't know how fucking long."

"Honestly, I don't want to speak to none of y'all. Y'all are forcing this on me. You know I don't need this shit, so why the fuck am I here?"

"Your nasty-ass attitude is the reason why we are here. You need help, Saiyah, and I'm not going to keep arguing with you. But since you wanna keep on doing this, here goes the paper to sign over your rights to Macayla since you think she is a joke."

The papers were signing over her rights temporarily to Erian. Maceo didn't think it was right to be signed over to him just yet.

"Seriously, Maceo, you want me to sign over my rights to my daughter?"

"I dealt you your cards, now it's your choice to fold or deal in. Which one are you doing?"

"I don't want to go, Maceo. They are going to bring all this stuff up that's irrelevant. I don't want to talk about it."

"Saiyah, you need help. I can't help you, so this is your only option right now. The shit you think is irrelevant is really relevant, so I need you to get it in your head. This is non-negotiable."

"Maceo, this isn't fair. You're taking me away from my baby. She's all I have," she cried.

"What about me? Or Mario? Or Erian? Or Ms. Erin? I love you, Saiyah, but you need help, baby. You're on the verge of a mental breakdown, and I can't have you around Macayla or anybody else when it happens."

"No, I'm not, Maceo. I'm fine. I'll do better. Don't make me go in there."

"Prove you not. Tell me he was lying when he said that you wanted it. You liked how that nigga was fucking you, right? You like how he ate you out. Ain't that what you told him? You told him you loved him."

The entire time, Saiyah was shaking her head, but she was getting angry. I could see it in her eyes that she was mad. The nurses for this expensive-ass rehab Maceo was putting her in were walking down the stairs.

Maceo owned the rehab that he was putting her in. A couple years back, Maceo had the biggest mental breakdown I had ever seen anybody have. Instead of shunning the whole world like most people do, the nigga did his research, brought in the best people to help him outta the situation, then bought them the building and let them construct it how they saw fit. He gave them the platform to help all those who needed it, from homeless, mentally disabled people to celebrities. I saw how it helped him, so I knew if it could help him, then it could help Saiyah.

Watching the interaction between the two, I knew it was a matter of time before I saw Saiyah reach across and punch Maceo dead in his shit, but she didn't stop. She was giving it to his ass, and that nigga ain't do shit but protect his face. Ol' pretty-boy-ass nigga.

"Fuck you, Drew. I ain't never wanted shit from you. You raped me. You told me that you would kill my daughter if I didn't. Why would you do that? I've never done anything to you. I hope you die, bitch. You made me get that abortion, and I'll never be able to have kids again, all because you raped me. Fuck you," she screamed as Maceo stopped shielding his face and grabbed her hands, shaking her.

"Saiyah! Stop, baby, stop! Yah! Yah Yah!" he called out, and she froze in place before she looked around at us.

Erian was watching in shock as it all went down. After Saiyah realized what happened, she tried to open the door, but Maceo stopped her. Erian had come out of her trance and was crying into my side, burying her face.

"I love you, Saiyah. On my mama, I do, bae, but you're not stable. Look at you."

He pulled her back and let her look at herself in the visor mirror. She just completely broke down. By the time she could talk to Maceo, the nurses, along with the director, were at the door.

"I love you guys! I'm sorry. I don't know what happened. Can you guys forgive me? Please," she cried with her hands shielding her eyes.

Erian was quietly leaning into my side as she cried for Saiyah. I looked up at my brother, and for the first time in a long time, Maceo had tears coming down his cheeks. That let me know right there how much he loved Saiyah. I always knew he loved Saiyah, just not how deep it was.

"Yah." His voice cracked.

She looked up at Maceo and threw herself in his arms. From there, I watched my brother go through his own breakdown for Saiyah. The windows were heavily tinted so they couldn't see in the car. They knew who Maceo was because he owned the place.

The two cried together, and I just rocked back and forth with Erian, but I felt they needed to cut their time short. "Mace, she gotta go, bro. They're waiting for her."

He nodded his head and pried Saiyah from him. "I love you, Yah. Ain't no bitch out here could touch you.

No matter who I'm with or what I'm doing, my heart ain't never beat for nobody but you. You my life, you and Macayla, and I would die for y'all. But you gotta do this, bae. You gotta find your way back to you—hood girl who would throw hands with her ma, and boss chick who was trying to get it on her own. Saiyah, who wanted to run the world with her man. Saiyah, who's the mother of Macayla. Grind for you and her. Get you some peace inside your head, ma, because this ain't you, and you know it. I love you. You always had my heart, and you always will," he told her before he leaned over and kissed her.

A knock came on the door, and Saiyah opened it. "I'll see y'all in three months or before. I love you, Maceo. Kiss my baby for me. Mario, I love y'all. Erian, I'm sorry."

"I love you, too, sis. Get better."

She nodded her head and got out of the car. The director introduced herself, and they walked off. I saw Maceo looking at the steering wheel, and I knew he was getting himself back in focus.

"She gon' be good, bro. Let's go back to the crib, take Macayla to Chuck E. Cheese, and chill for the remainder of the day."

He nodded his head. put the car in drive, and we pulled off.

For the remainder of the day, we all put on this fake charade as if we were happy, but I know it was eating at Maceo and Erian the most. Their smiles never quite reached their eyes, but for Macayla, they made it count.

I just prayed that once Saiyah got out, she was the old Saiyah, or an even better version of that Saiyah.

Chapter 19

Saiyah

A month later . . .

"Saiyah, you've been here for a month, and you haven't talked about much. You're vague with everything. Why is that?"

I looked at the therapist and wanted to smack the piss outta her. She had been trying to get me to talk, but I didn't know what to say or where to start.

"I don't have much to say. What is it that you want to know?"

"When did everything go bad for you? It seems that everything was good up until you got pregnant. You lost your boyfriend, you were still pregnant, and he didn't know, and your parents caused you to lose your scholarships. Speaking of parents, how is your relationship with them?"

"What parents? Those fake-ass people aren't my parents. They caused me to lose my entire life behind the bullshit they believed in. They claimed to be saints, but they were sinners just like me. They didn't have a fucking thing going for themselves but wanted to talk about me. The day they contacted Duke, my life ended."

"But your life didn't end. Why didn't you just go to another college?"

"My parents are professors and preachers. They don't believe in pre-marital sex, let alone a baby. They destroyed my credibility with every college I applied to. It was like word spread like wildfire. I started working at the local pharmacy store, and that's how I provided for myself and my daughter. My parents put all my stuff on the street a week later. I claimed my things and never looked back."

"So, they are unaware of Macayla's existence?"

"I would assume so."

"Maybe you should call your parents and see what they say. If they are still the same people that you knew, then sever all ties permanently, but if they have changed maybe, you can make amends."

I laughed at her because she clearly didn't know my parents.

"What seems to be funny?"

"You are thinking my parents would actually talk to me. Those saved, sanctified, and Holy Ghost-filled people would never talk to the daughter who embarrassed them."

"Well, how about we try? What is their number?"

I recited the number to her, and she called them, putting them on speaker phone.

"We're going to try a different approach for them."

I nodded my head.

"Hello." I heard my mother's voice come through the phone.

"Hi, this is Janice Taylor from John Stroger's Hospital. We believe we have a Saiyah Brady here. She's been in our morgue for a little over two weeks. Is there a way that you can come identify her body?"

"Howard! Howard! They say our baby is dead, Howard. I knew that I shouldn't have let you put her out," my mother cried.

My heart softened a little bit.

"Shelly, hush up and hand me the phone. Hello, who is this?"

"As I've told your wife, I'm Janice Taylor, and I'm from John Stroger's Hospital. I believe we have a Saiyah Brady in our morgue. She's been here for about two weeks now. We wanted to know could you come identify her."

"No! Not my baby girl. I didn't want this for Saiyah. Please, miss, tell me you're lying."

"Actually, I am not. Saiyah was found on the streets. She had been homeless for some time. She decided to end her life about two weeks ago. She even wrote a suicide letter. It is penned to you both."

"We loved Saiyah and just wanted her to learn her lesson. We thought she would've come back home, but we hadn't heard from her in almost six years. Did she have the baby? Do you know where he/she is at?"

I heard my mother crying in the background.

"Unfortunately, there is no way to know if she did until the autopsy is done. What time will you be down here to identify her?"

"We can be down there within an hour. Is there anything else that we need to know?"

"Yes! This is Janice Taylor from the Our People of Help Organization. I'm sitting here across from your daughter, Saiyah. She is in here seeking help because of underlying issues that you two have caused. Is there anything you would like to say to her?"

"Saiyah, baby, are you there?"

"Daddy!" I cried out.

"Saiyah, baby, I'm so sorry for how I treated you. We are sorry for how we treated you. Is there anything we can do to help your process?"

I looked at Janice skeptically. "Yes, I have a family therapy session coming soon. I would like you guys to attend. It's in two days. Will you be able to come?"

"Yes, we'll be there, sweetie. We love you, Saiyah, and we're sorry for all the damage we've done."

"I love you guys too."

Janice picked up the phone and gave them the address. I didn't know what to do, but I was excited about seeing them. Hopefully, the act that just happened on the phone would be what they really felt.

"So, how did it feel to hear how they felt about you?" she asked me.

"Good. I just want an apology from them both. I feel as though they owe me an apology for the things that they've done to me. I hope I can get it."

"I hope you do, too. Well, our session for today is over. I'll see you on Thursday."

Everyone just sat around looking at each other. It must've been awkward for them to be here, but I wouldn't be here if it weren't for them in the first place. My therapist, Janice, looked around at us before she spoke.

"Mr. and Mrs. Brady, I'm so glad that you could meet with us. Saiyah tells me that you guys have a strained relationship. Do you want to elaborate?"

"I'll begin. Saiyah is our oldest child, and I love her, but we've been keeping a secret from her," my father said.

"What's this secret you've been keeping from me?" I looked around at my parents and Janice.

My mother spoke up first. "Saiyah, we've never wanted you. You're adopted, and the only reason I took you in was because your real mother died and left you to me. I'm your aunt. I know it seems bad that I didn't want you, but she died of cancer and gave me custody of you. She left you behind three insurance policies. I have 'em here with me, along with the number to the lawyer you need to contact," she said, rummaging around in her purse.

For a minute, I sat there, letting everything register.

"Wait! Wait! You're my aunt and you're my uncle. Why didn't y'all tell me? I always knew I didn't fit in. Juju and Mimi both told me about y'all house y'all had in the suburbs. I never did a fucking thing for y'all to treat me that way. I never asked for anything. I went to school and came home like y'all asked. If y'all didn't want me, y'all should've let me fucking leave with Maceo when he told y'all I could live with him. You threw me out of the house when I was pregnant, and y'all didn't want a fucking thing to do with me. You should have given me my fucking money when you threw me out and destroyed my college career. Now, since I know the truth, I'm going to tell y'all how I feel about both of y'all."

"Wait one second. You're going to respect my wife."

"I'm not going to do a mothafucking thing. Fuck you and that bitch. And since y'all so fucking sanctified and holy, Uncle Fucking No Good, tell Auntie Bitch how you been fucking Sister Kelly for the longest. And Dearest Auntie, tell your husband that neither of those kids are his with his sterile ass. Juju and Mimi real daddy is a student she was fucking. Hand me my shit, and fuck both of y'all. And I expect to get a call from both Juju and Mimi soon, or I'll expose y'all, fake-ass preacher and First Lady. Y'all ain't shit," I snapped, reaching my hand out for my document.

She pulled out a yellow folder and handed it to me. Snatching it from her, I opened it. My mother's birth and death certificates, along with her obituary, my birth certificate, bank booklets, an insurance policy, and the number to the lawyer.

"Well, then, if there isn't anything else to say, this session is over."

"I got two things to ask. Why and how?"

"Why? How? What?" my uncle asked.

"Why the fake-ass shows the other day when you thought I was dead. You've never genuinely cared about me, so why the Academy Award performance? And how did I ruin your life?"

"Regardless of how I felt about you, you're my niece, and I love you, just not in the way I'm supposed to. I don't have any attachment to you. I didn't want any children yet. You ruined my life, so I made it a mission to ruin yours."

"You think you've ruined my life?" I asked, laughing. "The man you think left me all those years ago is back in my life. My daughter is healthy and thriving. On top of that, I'm going back to school. It might not be Duke or a prestigious school, but trust me, I'm going to be all that and more. And just for further information, I'll see you both in court. You're going to pay me back every dime that the Duke scholarship was going to award me. And, since I didn't have the money to attend school, and you destroyed my name throughout the academic community, I'm going to get back what you took. Have a nice life."

"You little bitch," my aunt snapped.

"Ah, ah, ah. I would stop if I was you. You've said more than enough. You're dismissed."

"I hope that man destroys your life," she said.

"Don't be so quick to throw stones while living in a glass house. Have a nice life, Auntie," I said with a smirk I knew would piss her off.

She grabbed her purse and stormed off. My uncle just sat there.

"Why are you still here?" I asked him.

"I honestly wanted to apologize. I never thought she hated you, just that she didn't want the responsibility. I'm so sorry, Saiyah, and I do wish we could've had a different relationship. If it's alright with you, I would still like to try and be a father to you and a grandfather to Macayla. Yes, I know her name. Juju follows you on social media."

I thought about it for a minute. He had never treated me wrong. On numerous occasions, he went behind my aunt's back to right the wrong she had done. He had always treated me like his, up until that day he found out I was pregnant. I think he was more disappointed than anything. I could forgive him in due time, but my auntie, I was going to make that bitch pay.

"Give me some time to think on it."

"I wouldn't have it any other way. Here's my cell and work numbers. If you ever wanna talk, I'm a call away," he said, giving me the card.

I stood up and gave him a hug. He kissed my forehead and let me go.

Sitting back down, I was happy. After my aunt revealed what she needed, I was elated. God don't like ugly, and He ain't too fond of cute.

"How are you feeling, Saiyah?"

"Like a burden has been lifted off my shoulders. Is my session over? I would like to call Macayla and Maceo."

"Sure. I think you handled it well. Couldn't have been my aunt. I would've beat her ass. You better than me, boo."

I laughed at her as I walked out of the room and to the phone. Somebody called my name. Turning around, I saw that it was my uncle. I stopped to see what he wanted. He came over to me and stopped.

"Do you think we can have lunch sometime tomorrow? I would really like to talk to you about some things that I need to tell you."

I contemplated telling him no, but something was telling me to talk to him.

"Tomorrow, here, around two. Is that good for you?"

"Yes, that's great. Thank you, Saiyah. You'll love to hear what I have to say," he said, giving me a hug and a kiss on the cheek before walking out.

The next day . . .

I headed down to our private meeting room on my floor. My uncle was waiting with my favorite food, homemade ribs, with fries and coleslaw. Sitting down next to him, I gave him a hug and dug into my food.

"Your mother, Surai, was the most beautiful woman I had ever laid eyes on. You look a lot like her. Everything about you reminds me of her, and I'll never forgive myself for what I did to her. It's all my fault that she isn't here with you today."

I stopped eating my food and looked at him. "What are you talking about, Uncle Howard?"

"That's another thing. I'm not your uncle, but your dad. I was married to your mother, Surai. We had been together for years. She was the only woman I truly loved. Well, at least to me she was. She didn't believe that, all because of your jealous-ass aunt. Shelly is the worst type of female. I hate her ass so much," he practically spat.

"What happened to my mom? Why do you blame yourself for her death?"

"We were driving home from dinner when your aunt called her with these false accusations that I was cheating on her. I wasn't, by the way, but she kept all these lies going to your mother. Your mother hung up with her, and we argued. During the drive, I stopped looking at the road and ended up plowing into a wall. Your mother wasn't wearing her seat belt and was ejected from the car. I survived, but I was pinned in the car, crushing my private areas. I was told that I would never be able to have kids again. I would be sterile for the rest of my life.

"Your mother left you to your aunt if something was to happen to the both of us. You were only two and a half when the accident occurred. After the incident, I stayed away from you until you were about five, and that's when I started coming back around. Your aunt blackmailed me into not telling you.

"I wasn't your average nine-to-five working man. I sold drugs for a living, and that's how I made a lot of my money. I put your mother through nursing school because that was her dream," he said, looking at me somberly.

I pulled my hands out of his. "Why didn't you stop her when she ruined my college career?"

"Your auntie is very powerful in the academic world, and I also didn't want to go to jail. I swear, I wanted to tell you, but I thought you would hate me, Saiyah. If I could go back, I would rather live my life knowing you hate me and know the truth than live this lie. I missed so much important shit in your life. I regret the decision to agree to her terms via blackmailing me."

"I accept your apology. I've spent so much time mad at the two of you that it nearly destroyed my life. All can be forgiven if you do me a favor."

"Anything for you."

"Kill Erian's stepfather. I want him wiped off the map. If you love me and want my forgiveness, you'll do it."

"Drew? What did that mothafucka do?"

"He's raped me for the last five years. I want him dead, Daddy. Kill him for me. And he's the reason I can't have any more kids. He forced me to get an abortion when I was too far along. I didn't want to do it, but he forced me, and I had no one to run to. You have to kill him, Daddy!" I cried real tears. I did want Drew dead, and I knew I was playing on my dad's guilt, but I refused to put Maceo in that position. But Daddy could do it. He owed me that much.

"I'll do it, baby girl. Just give me some time. When can I meet Macayla, my granddaughter? She looks just like Maceo."

"You can meet her whenever you get ready. And you need to hold a conversation with Maceo again. He and I are trying to get our lives back on track. He's the reason I'm in here. He has helped me get back to the person I am. I'm just elated that he's taken the time out to show me what is real and what isn't."

"I'm not going to lie. I knew who Maceo was before you started talking to him. Now, I didn't know about you and him, you know, but I had an idea. Y'all were damn near joined at the hip. I didn't like it because he was older than you. I knew you were much happier with him than alone. When you told me that you were pregnant, I was crushed. My heart was broken because I wanted more for you. Instead of leaving you high and dry, I should've embraced you, and I'm sorry for that. I'll never stop telling you how sorry I am for that. I just want a chance to right my wrongs."

I listened to him as he spoke, and I knew he was genuine. I loved him, and I couldn't deny that if I wanted to. "Dad, you're forgiven, but I need to be getting back to my room. Our time is up," I said to him. Grabbing the leftovers from my food, I closed the container and wiped my hands off.

"Can we set a date so I can see Macayla once you're out of here?"

"We sure can. I have your number, and all you have to do is call the front desk, and they'll direct your call."

"Ok, sweetheart. Give your old man a hug."

I gave him a hug, and we separated.

"Keep doing good, Saiyah. Don't let anything or anyone get in your way. Destroy everyone who interrupts your happiness. If you need me, you got my number." With that, he kissed me on the cheek and walked out.

I felt good about our conversation. I never knew my aunt hated me so much that she would do such a thing, but there was one thing I needed to know. Running out of the room, I called his name and beckoned for him to come back.

"What's wrong?"

"How did you end up marrying my aunt?"

"I wouldn't marry that bitch if it was my last resort. She had her last name changed. I would have sex with her every now and then and put on the charade that we were together, but I didn't want her. My woman is the hoe you were talking about in church. I'll bring her to meet you when you're up to it."

"I'm sorry about that, too, but if you would've told me the truth, this wouldn't have happened."

"You're right, but let me get out of here. I'll see you soon," he said, rushing off.

I turned around and was headed to my room when one of the nurses stopped me.

"Hey, Saiyah, Maceo just came looking for you. He's in your room, and hunty, that man must really love you. Let me be quiet before I give away too much."

"Maceo is here?"

She nodded, smiling.

Maceo had my room on a private wing. There were only two bedrooms on each side of that wing, and I had the biggest one. Walking into my room, I saw roses that led to the bedroom. Hands went around my waist, and I smelled Maceo.

"You know I ain't never did nothing like this before."

"Really? All of this is for me?"

"Yeah, who else? Come on so I can give you a massage." There was a massaging table with various oils on the side. Maceo helped me out of my clothes and onto the table.

Removing his shirt, he grabbed one of the oils, poured it into his hands, and started massaging it into my skin.

"When you get out, I think we should take a family vacation. Macayla misses you," Maceo said.

"I miss my baby, too. Is she behaving?"

"Hell, yeah. Too good if you ask me. She had me playing tea party with her the other day. Mario's ass walked in, and she suckered him into it, bae. I promise you that nigga was enjoying himself too much."

I cracked up laughing because the visual of them two playing tea party was comical.

"Did you have fun?"

"Anything for my li'l lady. Her birthday is coming up soon, and I wanted to know what you wanted to do for it."

"She's always wanted to go to Disney World, so I think we should take her."

"Yeah, I was thinking of inviting Li'l Mace, too."

"That's fine. He is her brother."

I moaned as he massaged my booty cheeks.

"Damn, I ain't know I had the magic touch," he said, laughing.

"You do. Yo' hands better not graze my lips no more."

"I ain't even touch yo' pussy, though," he said, chuckling.

"Lying ass. If you wanna touch it, daddy, that's all you gotta say."

Flipping me over on my back, he spread my legs and rubbed his nose in my honey pot. "That shit smell good. You gon' let me taste it?"

"I can't stop you," I told him.

"I'll do that later, but I got a surprise for you. You down for it?" He looked at me to make sure.

"Okay."

He walked into the bathroom and came out with a girl dressed up in a Swarovski diamond outfit.

I sat up and looked at him. "What's this, Maceo?"

"Jasemine, this is Saiyah. Saiyah, this is Jasemine. She's one of my girls that works for the modeling agency."

"Ok, and?"

"Well, she's here to get you ready for your photo shoot, so go in the bathroom and let her help you get ready. This is stage one of your process to seeing your beauty on the outside since you've found it on the inside. You've worked towards it, baby. You're embracing it and you're almost there, bae. Keep going."

I leaned in toward him, placing a kiss on his lips. I got up and went into the bathroom, to take a shower and wash my hair. I got out of the shower, sat in the chair, and waited for Jasemine.

She walked in with a rack of clothes for me. "Maceo has spared no expense for you. He asked that whatever you want, you get. How would you like your hair?"

"I don't know. Make it match the outfit. I want the one you had on."

"Are you sure? Maceo told me to have you pick anything you want, but you must be comfortable."

"I'm comfortable in my own skin. And for once, I'm happy about it." I smiled at her, and she smiled back. I could tell that it was genuine, and I appreciated it.

"You have some very beautiful skin as well as a beautiful body. Do you mind me asking you some questions?"

"No, ask whatever you please."

"Does this place really help?"

I thought about it for a minute, then answered. "You know, when I came here a month ago, I was against the entire idea, but as the days went on, I was getting the breaks that I deserved and absorbing information that soothed my aching soul. If Maceo hadn't forced me to come, there's no telling what I would've done. I love Maceo and our daughter, and I've been through so much.

I just want to get back to Saiyah, get back to loving and living carefree. I knew the issues started with my parents, but I didn't have the push I needed to. Today, I got that push, and I hope for their sake and mine that what they said matches up with their actions. I cut them out of my life before, and I have no problem doing it again."

"Wow! I wish I had a man who loved me as much as Maceo loves you."

"You can't love somebody else if you don't love yourself. Beauty is both on the inside and out, but you have to find your inner beauty before your outer beauty can be seen."

"Is it alright if I take it personal with you?"

"Sure. It's from your lips to my ears." I smiled at her in the mirror as she continued to blow-dry my hair.

"I've been in love before, or at least I thought it was, but Hurt was a different breed. His actions and words came through his hands. It was never simple with him, and if I could rewind time, I would. I met him so young, and he took advantage of that. When I finally got the chance to break away, I did. I promised to never return. That was five years ago, and I'm tired of looking over my shoulder. Still to this day, I'm hiding from him. I'm afraid that one day, my inner scars will start showing, and I'll be to the point of no return," she said, taking a paranoid looking around the room.

Grabbing her arm, I pulled her in front of me. I took the blow dryer and set it on the counter.

"Jasemine, how old is Hurt, and how old are you?"

"You honestly want to know my age?"

I nodded yes.

"I'm nineteen, but please don't tell Maceo. He wanted someone over twenty-one, and I lied to him. This is how I make a living."

"Calm down. I wouldn't tell Maceo. But you didn't answer how old Hurt was."

"I met him when I was twelve. He was twenty-one. Hurt swore he loved me and would never do anything to hurt me. I was heartbroken when I found out he had a girlfriend and she was pregnant. I tried to run, but Hurt told me he would kill me. For two years, I endured the torture that he put me through. One day, he decided that I should have sex with his friends. My answer was no. He tried to attack me, but I grabbed his gun and shot him. I don't know if I killed him or not. I just grabbed the money he had and hauled ass.

"I watched and searched the news every day, looking to see if anybody found him, and I haven't heard anything. Once I got away from him, I used the fake ID he had made and got in school, and from there, I'm where I'm at now. I'm happy where I'm at. I just know Hurt is going to come for me one day, and my life will be over."

"Live, Jasemine. Don't let life stop you from being happy. Be carefree, turn up! Love you, beautiful scars and all. Let that be the testimony you tell when you've made it. Don't let fear stop you from living life. I allowed embarrassment and shunning from the world to stop me, but never again. Live like you've never lived before. Love will always find its way to the right one. Trust and believe it, boo. Now, stop crying. You supposed to be making me look as beautiful as you."

She laughed at me as she wiped her tears with the tissue I handed her.

"Thank you, Saiyah. I appreciate it. But let's get you finished and ready. Your photo shoot is going to be so beautiful. Maceo went all out. A queen is simply what you are to that man."

I blushed as I thought about what she said. I loved Maceo, and that man treated me like royalty when we were together the first time, and now that I was working on myself, he'd been there every step of the way. I couldn't have asked for a better man in my life. I just wished we hadn't wasted so much time over a misunderstanding.

I closed my eyes as I let her do her magic.

"You can open your eyes now."

I opened my eyes, and I couldn't believe it. She gave me a complete makeover. My hair, nails, and makeup were done to perfection. I pulled her into a tight hug as I looked at myself in the mirror.

"Thank you, Jasemine."

"You can call me Minnie, and no, thank you. But we need to get going, so throw on this robe, and I'll carry the outfits I think would best suit you, and we can go."

I took the robe and put it on as she grabbed the outfits and shoes. "Let's go. Maceo is waiting on us."

I walked out behind her as we went into the awaiting van. We got inside and closed the door. The driver pulled off, and we headed to the photo shoot.

I was excited for the first time in a long time. I couldn't wait to see Maceo.

Chapter 20

Maceo

Sitting in the chair as ol' girl cut my hair, I thought about Saiyah and how happy she was today. She was getting back to the old Saiyah, and I loved watching her transform. Her therapist said that she had three more sessions and she could come home soon. I was going to throw my baby a big-ass party just to show her love.

Saiyah was my li'l hitta back in the day. If I swung, so did Saiyah, and baby girl had those hands. She would be fighting niggas with me. Yeah, I was older than Saiyah, but she was my li'l G. She was tougher than a lot of these pussy-ass niggas today. Had a heart of gold, but fierce like a lion. Saiyah ain't let too much get in her head. I knew that night when dude bitch ass said that shit, it was going to affect Saiyah. I watched the light leave her eyes when he said it, and it was confirmed when I got in her head in the truck that morning. The thing that broke my heart the most was that she had an abortion and might not be able to have kids ever again. I at least wanted four more kids outta her. Yes, a nigga wanted a big-ass family, and I was going to make it happen.

Checking my phone, I saw a text from Jasemine saying that they were on their way. Telling everybody to get in place, I walked to the door and slid it open. The van rolled in and stopped. Pushing the door back closed, I went to the passenger door and opened it. Jasemine stepped down, then Saiyah. I had to stop myself from licking my lips. Baby girl was thick in that robe.

"Thank you, baby," Saiyah said, coming over and giving me a kiss on the lips.

"You're welcome. Go get ready for the shoot," I said, kissing her back. She walked off behind Jasemine, and I had to will my dick to go down. She had me brick from that one kiss.

Adjusting myself, I headed over to the dressing room to wait on Jasemine to come. About fifteen minutes later, she was coming through, grabbing my clothes, and rushing me to get dressed. After I got dressed, I headed out to where Saiyah was already in her shoot. My mouth damn near dropped to the floor when I saw the outfit she had on. The Swarovski diamond outfit that was like what Jasemine had on earlier looked a hunnid times better on Saiyah as she posed for the camera and listened to the directions of the photographer. I had to admire her beauty. I could see that she was genuinely happy and loving the shoot. That's why I did it for her, so she could see that her inner beauty equated to her outer beauty. I wanted to make her feel like the only woman in the world.

"Maceo, you're up," Jasemine said behind me.

Walking up behind Saiyah, I buried my face in the crook of her neck as I placed subtle kisses on it. Flipping her around, I looked down in her face as she lightly panted.

"I love you, Yah."

"I love you too, Mace."

"Maceo and Saiyah, can you get on the floor? Mace, prop up a leg, and Saiyah, slowly crawl toward Maceo."

We followed what he told us. After a few more poses and an outfit change, we were down to our final outfit change, and I knew Saiyah was going to be shocked. Saiyah didn't know I had her dream wedding dress made along with my matching tux.

I made it out before she did, and I had the scene set, along with the wedding ring that she wanted. It cost me a cool three milli, but for Saiyah, I'd buy the world if I had to.

Standing underneath the arch, I waited for her to come out as I hyped myself up to propose to the woman I loved. Erian and Mario had just shown up and stood off to the side.

"Ahhhhh! She looks so beautiful."

I turned around and looked at Saiyah. I swear my heart stopped beating.

"Maceo, what is this? How did you get this dress designed? Like, what is going on?" She looked around and noticed Erian and Mario. By the time she turned around, I was already down on one knee.

"Maceo! No! No! I know this isn't what I think it is," she said, stepping back from me.

I pulled her toward me. "I know when we linked back up, shit just wasn't the same, but standing before me is the woman I fell in love with, the one I wanted to marry and spend the rest of my life with. I told you my heart don't beat for anybody but you and my kids. Standing before you today, I ask that you allow me to be the man that you need, love you like you need, and cherish you like you deserve, and give you the world you've always wanted. Let me be your Superman and save you from all harm. Can I be that, Yah? Will you marry me, Saiyah Heiress Brady?"

"Yes! Yes! Yes, I'll marry you, De'Maceo Santana Perkins."

I heard the camera taking shots as I stood up and pulled Saiyah into a kiss. "I love you, Yah. I promise to make it worth it. Just let me show you that I can love you beyond the hurt you've experienced."

"You're already showing me," she said, pulling me into a kiss.

By the time we left the shoot, it was nightfall. Saiyah had to return to the program, but I didn't want to leave her.

"Yah, how about I spend the night with you? Just for tonight."

"You'll be there in the morning when I wake up?"

"Where I'ma go? But let's get you back. I don't want you to get in trouble."

"Maceo, you own the place. How much trouble can I get in?"

I laughed at it because she was right. "That don't matter. Let's get you back, bae."

I helped her into the van, got in behind her, and we rode all the way back to the rehab. I thought about changing my mind, but I knew that Saiyah wouldn't have it. We arrived at the rehab spot forty-five minutes later. I helped her out, and we walked inside.

Getting to her bedroom door, I stopped her in front of it. For me to be twenty-eight, I was nervous as fuck like it was my first time.

"Why you look nervous?"

"Man, I ain't been with you in years. I feel like we are going back to our first time."

"De'Maceo Santana, you know I'm not a virgin. Besides, if we are going back to first times, I cried that night, remember?"

"Hell, yeah. Swore I was going to leave you."

"Well, yo' ass can't leave me now. We together forever."

"Forever? Is that so, Mrs. Perkins?"

"Hell, yeah. We foreva, in my Cardi B voice."

Laughing at her, I leaned her up against the door as my hands traveled underneath her dress. "Why you ain't got no panties on, woman?"

"I mean, you said you wanted to taste it later. It's later. You still want to?"

Licking my lips, I pushed open her room door and led us back toward the bed. Bending down, I removed her shoe as I licked up her leg. Removing the other shoe, I repeated the same pattern, but this time, I reached her center. I could feel the heat radiating from it.

"You sure you wanna go there?"

She nodded her head. Raising her dress over her hips, I pulled her to the end of the bed, pushing her legs back as far as they could go. I traced my tongue down her slit before I dived in face-first and ate my dessert.

"Mmmmaceooo!" she moaned out as I unleashed my tongue lashing on her. Her juices were all over my face and tongue, and I couldn't get enough of it. Sucking on her clit like I was sucking through a straw, I kept eating her sweet Georgia peach until she came all over my tongue, and I swallowed it down. It tasted as sweet as her.

Releasing her legs and listening to her panting, I pulled my pants off along with my shirt. She quickly removed her dress and lay in the middle of the bed. Getting on the bed, I hovered over her, taking in every inch of her body in the moonlight. Her body was everything to me. Her titties sat up high, and her stomach was flat as a board.

"Yah, I'ma ask one last time. Are you sure?"

Wrapping her legs around my waist, she pulled me until I was lined up with her center. "I want you, Maceo.

Just for tonight, can you make me feel good? You've had me on a high all day long, and I don't wanna come down just yet."

"Say no more."

She guided me into her. Her walls gripped the top of my dick. Pushing a little harder, I eased my way in. Looking down at Saiyah, her eyes were snapped shut.

"Open yo' eyes, Yah."

Her eyes opened and connected to mine as I slowly slid in and out of her.

Leaning down, I kissed her lips and pulled back because I felt something wet on my face. Looking at Yah, I saw the tears sliding down. Stopping, I looked down at her.

"Don't stop, Maceo. Please," she begged me.

Leaning down again, I pulled her into a tight hug as I drilled inside of her. Her fingernails were digging into my skin.

"Tell me you love me, Yah," I groaned against her neck. Placing kisses on her neck, I felt her body shiver.

"I love you, Maceo." Her legs wrapped around my body, pulling me into her. Her lips grazed my neck before she kissed and licked my spot.

"Fuckkk!" I yelled out as Yah's body rocked back and forth with mine. Drawing back, I flicked my tongue across her nipples before sucking on them like a gumdrop.

"Mmmmmm!" Saiyah's body shivered again. "I wanna ride, Maceo."

Flipping us over, I let her adjust to me as she slowly slid up and down. Yah's pussy was a death trap.

"Ride this dick like it's yours, Yah."

Looking down at me, she smiled, then rode me like her life depended on it.

"Maceo, I'm about to cum," she yelled out as she picked up her speed.

"Fuck! Slow down, Yah," I groaned out as I felt my nut rising.

"Maceoooooo!" she yelled out as she came. I followed behind her, filling her up with all my kids.

"Fuck, Yah. What the fuck?" I looked at her.

"Maceo, tell me you wore a condom."

I looked at her ass like she was crazy. "Hell, nah. You mine. Besides, I ain't had sex in like three months. I'm clean."

She looked at me suspiciously and scared at the same time.

"What's up, Yah? What's wrong?"

"Maceo, I can't have kids. The doctor I went to said that I couldn't."

"Remember that conversation about faith. You better start having some because I believe that you can. If you want, I'll pay for us both to get checked out."

"You know you can have kids. You have Li'l Maceo."

"And Li'l Maceo is about to be four, so I don't know if I can have kids. Besides, if it makes my future wife happy, then I'm for it."

"I love you, De'Maceo. I really appreciate you." She yawned.

"I love you, too, Yah, but you need to get in the shower, bae."

She nodded her head before rolling out of the bed and walking to the bathroom.

"You are coming?" she asked seductively.

She didn't have to ask me twice. I hopped out and followed her into the bathroom and got round two popping in the shower and then round three on the counter. The Saiyah I knew was back.

The next morning, I woke up feeling as though somebody was watching me. Grabbing the remote to open the blinds, I saw someone sitting on the edge of the bed. Sitting up, I tapped Saiyah, and she sat up on alert with me. When the blinds finally opened, I saw Tee sitting on the bed, staring into space.

"What the fuck? Tee, why you in Saiyah's room?"

"I came to have a conversation with her. Why are you here?"

"Get the fuck out, Tee. It's too early in the morning for this bullshit. Matter of fact, how the hell you get in here?"

Saiyah looked back and forth between us before going into the bathroom.

I walked over and yanked Tee off the bed but ended up dropping her right back when I saw the marks on her.

"I'll be damned. I put one baby mama in rehab for one thing, and the other one needs to go for being an addict."

"I'm not an addict, Maceo. I don't do drugs. What are you talking about?" she asked, rubbing up and down her arm. Strike one. She rubbed underneath her nose. Strike two. She hopped up and started pacing the room. Strike three.

"I wouldn't even be on drugs if it wasn't for you and that bitch, Maceo. You love her more than me. You've never even uttered that you've loved me," she snapped angrily.

Saiyah came out of the bathroom in her high school sweater, and I swear my body reacted to hers fast. She walked around to me and wrapped her arms around my waist.

"Baby, why is she still here?"

Tee looked at Saiyah, then me. She started to approach, but I stopped her.

"Yah, she on drugs, and I don't know what she on, baby."

"Babe, did you tell her about our engagement?"

As Tee was going off, Saiyah let me know that she had alerted the director and she was on her way over. I breathed a sigh of relief and hoped they would hurry the fuck up.

"You're going to marry her, Maceo? What about me? You've never loved me nor wanted me, so what's so special about her?"

I wasn't about to answer that. Saiyah just looked at me.

"Terina, is it? I think Maceo loves you, but not in the way that you want him to. Everybody is entitled to have someone love them unconditionally. I just don't believe that he's the one for you. Maybe there's someone who loves you unconditionally and would do anything for you. I assume that the man you're pregnant by isn't your boyfriend?"

"No, no, he is, but he doesn't love me. I was using him to get to Maceo, and he got me strung out on drugs. I've been trying to kick 'em on my own, but I couldn't. Ever since Maceo took everything from me, I've been trying to survive on my own."

Yah looked at me, and I let her know that she was doing good.

"Why did Maceo take all those things away from you?" Saiyah asked.

"Because he felt like as a woman, I should have my own instead of leeching off him. I love Maceo, but he doesn't see that."

"Tee, I know you love me, but I don't love you like that. You gave me my first son, and I'll always love you for that."

"I want more, Maceo, and I won't stop until I get it."

"Tee, after you have this baby, you will be going to jail, and I have to put up money that I shouldn't have to. Ever since you got pregnant with Li'l Maceo, you've been milking me for everything. That shit came to an end because I was paying for shit that didn't have to do with my son."

"What is going on in here? Miss, how did you get in here?" the director asked, and I was jumping for joy.

I was about to show Tee's ass what to do. I didn't trust her. She was up to some shit. If Saiyah was here alone, ain't no telling what she would've done.

"I was here visiting my sister and her man."

Saiyah looked at Tee with wide eyes before lunging for her. I grabbed her in time before she beat Tee's ass.

"You not my sister. You are a conniving bitch. And don't think I don't know why you here. Had Maceo not been here, you would've gotten yo' ass beat. Pregnant or not, you're up to something, and I don't trust a bitch who can lie with a straight face. Ms. Gwen, Maceo and I woke up, and she was sitting on the edge of the bed, rocking back and forth. On top of that, she pregnant and using drugs. Look at the track marks on her arm. She looks like she's laying tracks for Amtrak and Metra."

I wanted to laugh, but this was serious.

"Maceo, what do you want me to do?"

"Detox her and monitor the baby."

She nodded her head and called for two nurses. By then, Tee had dozed off as she stood up. Shaking my head, I waited for them to remove her before I looked at Yah.

"Come here, Yah," I said to her.

She came over to me, but she wouldn't look at me.

"Why you looking down, Yah? What's the issue?"

"Am I going to have to deal with her? I mean, we're engaged to be married, and I don't want any ties to her. And is that your baby?"

Now, I saw where she was going with this. "That's not my baby. Tee claimed we fucked, but I know for a fact that I didn't fuck her. That ain't my baby. Whoever her new nigga is, I don't know him. Tee ain't had Li'l Mace in a while. Her mother has him."

"So, get your son, Mace. He doesn't need that instability in his life."

"Alright. When you finish the program, we can go grab him. I want this shit forever, Yah. I want you to get these things out with your parents and come home."

She nodded her head, and I pulled her into a hug. I told her I had to get to this meeting, and I would talk to her later. Kissing her lips, I headed out the door, but before I went anywhere, I needed to talk to the director about Tee.

Chapter 21

Teriana "Tee"

Two weeks earlier . . .

De'Maceo Santana had been my nigga for the longest. At least, that's what I believed. He knew I trapped him, but that was the only way I could guarantee a spot in his life and pockets forever. Even though he stopped messing with me way before I told him about Li'l Maceo, I still wanted that nigga. I'd been trying to throw the pussy his way, but he was turning it down every chance that he got. I knew a couple of my home girls had fucked him, but all they were was a quick nut. Maceo loved me, and I knew he did. That was why he kept me laced in the latest shit, hair slayed, and money in my pockets. He could front all he wanted to, but Mace loved me. I just prayed that he never found out my li'l secret that I kept hidden from him.

Rolling me a blunt, I sat down on the couch with my home girl, FeFe. FeFe had been my bitch since we were kids, and I loved the fuck outta her, but she was too judgmental at times. Like now, her ass was telling me what I shouldn't be doing.

"Tee, you need to stop living off Mace. If that nigga gets killed today, what you gon' do?"

"Mace ain't gon' get killed, though. He doesn't do shit to get killed. I like having to not work and shit. I pushed his son out, so the least he could do is take care of me."

"So, because you pushed out Li'l Mace, you think Maceo is supposed to take care of you?"

I looked at her ass like "duh."

"Well then, you got the game fucked up. That man just gave you a month or so to get your shit together. It was a clear warning, and I would be listening if I was you. Niggas like Mace don't make threats that they don't follow through on," she said, taking the blunt from me and taking a pull from it.

My phone pinged, and I saw that it was a text from Mace.

Enjoy your freedom while you can, Teriana, because it's going to end soon.

I rolled my eyes so hard at his text because he was being so dramatic. Getting up, I looked at FeFe and saw that she was high as hell. Looking at her, I licked my lips. FeFe, whose real name was Ferrah, was so fucking pretty. She had the prettiest chocolate skin, big brown eyes, and a petite frame with a big ol' booty.

"Why you are looking at me like that, Tee?"

"Come on. You know what I want, Ferrah."

"You said that was a one-time thing," she said to me, but I could see that she wanted it.

Standing up, I went over to her and dropped down to the floor before pulling her to the edge and raising up her dress. I saw that her pussy was freshly shaved, and it was glistening with juices. Rubbing my fingers up and down it, I knew that she wanted it when I heard a moan escape her mouth.

Spreading her lips, I pulled her clit into my mouth, and that shit tasted like chocolate. I couldn't even control the moans that were escaping my mouth as I ate her sweet, juicy pussy. It wasn't long before her legs were trembling and shaking. She pulled my head in closer, and I took advantage of that. Slipping my fingers into her tight hole, I fingered her as she started cumming on my tongue. She tasted like heaven on my tongue.

"I'm not going to keep doing this with you, Tee," she said, coming down off that orgasmic high.

I smiled at her before stripping out of my clothes and climbing up on her face. She could stunt all she wanted to. She knew that she loved eating this pussy, and I enjoyed her doing it.

"Mmmmm, so you done eating this pussy, FeFe?" I asked her as she had a mouth full of my pussy, eating it like Sunday's dinner.

After she subtly shook her head no, I grabbed her head and started riding her face. I couldn't stop my eyes from rolling in the back of my head. She had given the best head so far, and I loved it.

"Fuck, Fe! You're about to make me cum, baby," I said, pulling her head in closer as the orgasm ripped through my body.

"Ahhhhh! Oh my fucking God!" I yelled out as I continued to ride her face. She was placing kisses all over my clit, and I couldn't take it anymore. Falling to the side, I saw that she was wiping her lips and smirking.

"You might as well head to the bedroom. It's about to be a long night."

I got up and did what she said. For the rest of the night, I enjoyed the pleasure that I received.

A few weeks later . . .

A few weeks had passed, and I was enjoying the freedom of not having Li'l Mace. I loved him, but I just didn't want any kids. He was my little cash cow. I had contemplated for a while on having an abortion, but by the time I wanted to go through with it, I was too far along with him. When I informed Maceo about it, I knew that he wasn't happy either. It didn't matter one way or another because I knew that having his child would have me financially secure, and I needed that. I was tired of punching the clock at the bank. It was alright for the li'l coins that I was making, but I needed real money, and that shit just wasn't enough. I wanted to look sexy as hell when I stepped out, not like I had been shopping in Rainbow. Hell, I turned up too much not to be fine as fuck in the club.

So, here I was shopping in the Gucci store, looking at the latest purses and shoes for my night out. I couldn't wait because tonight was the grand opening for Maceo's studio, and a bitch wanted to look fine as fuck for him. Maybe baby daddy might slip me some dick tonight. After grabbing the shoes and matching purse, I headed to the counter and handed the lady my black card that Maceo had given me.

"I'm sorry, Miss, but your card declined," she said, and I looked at her with wide eyes because this card didn't have a limit on it, so I was confused about why it was declined.

"Try it again because that card shouldn't decline at all."

"I tried it four times already. It says that you need to contact the bank," she told me, and I couldn't believe this shit.

Snatching my card from her, I left the store and called Maceo.

"Yo, what's up, Tee?"

"Maceo, my card declined. What the fuck is going on? Are we broke?" I asked him, on the verge of tears because this was embarrassing.

"No, *we* ain't a mothafucking thing. You're broke. I told yo' ass to enjoy your freedom, and I see that you have, seeing as you haven't called your fucking son. On top of that, I got the bill for last fucking month. Twenty-five thousand on what, Tee? None of that shit was for my son. All that shit was for you. You got me fucked up thinking that I'm your daddy and going to take care of your grown ass. You have two weeks to find a job and another place to stay. Your lease on your apartment is up next week, so get to packing," he said before hanging up the phone.

I pulled the phone from my ear, and I couldn't believe the shit that I had heard. Oh, that nigga was going to see me. I left the mall, heading to my Mercedes that he had copped for me, only to see that it was gone and replaced with a two-door Honda Civic. Getting closer to the window, I pulled the note off it.

Baby Mama,

The Mercedes was costing a nigga too much, so I had to return it. Here is your new car. I had it cleaned and detailed for you. You have a remote starter and security system on it. Hell, I even had them put tint on it. Please, take good care of it because this is your ride until you can afford a new one.

Your baby daddy,
Mace

I couldn't believe this mothafucka was really doing this shit. Pulling out my iPhone, I called him, but my service had been disconnected. Opening the car door, I saw the keys sitting on the seat with a Metro PCS bag. Reaching over and grabbing the bag, I saw that nigga had gotten me another phone. Picking it up, I saw a text message waiting on the screen.

Baby Mama, you've just received gift number two. Be careful with that iPhone. Drop that bitch and there is no way of replacing it. Oh, yeah, the bill is due on the 10th of every month, and it cost $78. Don't forget that. Your car insurance is due on the 15th of every month. It is $100. Don't forget these things because it's important. In the console, you have a pre-paid Chase card that I loaded five hundred dollars on. That's your child support for the month. Use it wisely. Sincerely, your petty-ass baby daddy.

Ugh, I couldn't fucking stand him. I couldn't believe that he was really doing me like this. After all the shit that I had put up with, this nigga was doing me dirty as fuck. I swear to God, I was fucking him up when I saw him. Ol' dirty-dick-ass nigga.

After Maceo stripped me of everything, my life spiraled down faster than I could catch it. The drugs and the secret lover were taking a toll on me, especially with me being pregnant. I tried to convince Mace that it was his baby, but he was no dummy. Now, I was left getting high with my new boo, while Maceo was happy and in love with his bitch.

I had been stalking them for the longest, and I couldn't believe he had her in a rehab and was that much in love with her, but I could see that he was happy. It broke my heart, but I was about to shatter hers. Once Maceo left for the night, I was going to pay her a visit.

Waking up, I felt weak and knew that my body was going through withdrawals. Feeling my stomach, I saw that I was still pregnant, but I hadn't felt my baby move since yesterday. Panicking, I got up and headed to the bathroom when I realized something. I wasn't at home and didn't know where I was at, until everything flooded back to me. I was in the rehab with Maceo and his li'l bitch. Turning around to head back to the bed, my body went straight to the floor.

The door opened, and a woman appeared. "Miss, are you alright? Nurse, we need the doctor in here," she yelled out as she helped me up and into the bed.

"I don't need a nurse or a damn doctor. I need to get out of here and get my son. What the fuck are you doing?" I asked as she started strapping me down to the bed while I fought her off.

"Miss, please stop fighting me. Nurse!" she called out again.

"Tee, calm down!" I heard Maceo say.

Turning to my left, I saw Maceo sitting there. I didn't see him there before, so where did he come from? I started calming down as I stared at him.

"Let me holla at her alone. I won't be long," he told the lady.

She nodded her head before walking out.

"What's up, Tee? When did you start using drugs?"

"It's not me! Lo is forcing drugs into my system, Maceo. I didn't know how to ask for help. I was embarrassed. Lo would kill me if he found out I was with you."

"Lo? Londo?"

I dropped my head in shame.

"Yo, you foul as fuck. My cousin, Tee. My fucking cousin. Lo is what? Eighteen? Why the fuck is you even fucking with him? Is this that nigga baby?"

I nodded my head.

"Damn, Tee. I knew that nigga was looking at me sideways whenever I brought yo' name up. You fucking that nigga knowing he don't even fuck with me."

I knew that Londo was jealous of Maceo. He had never liked Maceo and always claimed that Maceo and Mario were trying to be better than him and his brothers, but I knew that wasn't the case. I didn't even love Londo, but he loved the fuck outta me, and I couldn't leave him just yet.

"Tee, how the fuck did you really get that much cocaine?"

"We had just come from out west when Londo started acting crazy, swerving and shit. The police saw the shit and pulled us over. I didn't know the drugs were even in the car, but when Londo saw the police coming, he threw it in my purse. When they searched the car, they found the drugs. Londo instantly claimed it was mine, and being that I had track marks down my arm from the needles, they believed him. But with that much, I could've overdosed. I still can't believe that he lied on me, but I'm afraid of him, Maceo. He always threatens to kill you when I try to leave. I only stayed because I was protecting you."

I had to make up the lie to get in his good graces because if he knew the truth, he would go berserk.

"You had my son around him? Were you getting high around my son? Like what the fuck, Teriana? Are you stupid? What if them boys ran up in the house while my son was there? Like, do you not think?"

"I made a mistake, Maceo. Damn. I'm going to get better. I have a baby to take care of."

Maceo looked at me and dropped his head. "Tee, I gotta tell you something."

I could see the worry lines in his forehead as he opened his mouth to tell me.

"Tee, they couldn't find a heartbeat for the baby. I'm sorry."

I looked at him to be sure that this wasn't some joke. "You're joking, right?"

He shook his head.

"Mace, stop playing and be for real. What happened to the baby?"

"Tee, you're still carrying the baby. For them to get the baby out, you'll have to push. I'm sorry, ma. The heroin and coke in your system killed him. He couldn't handle it."

I couldn't believe what he was saying. My baby. He was dead. I didn't even know it was a he. I hadn't been back to the doctor since I was three months pregnant, and I was close to the seven-month mark now.

A part of me was sad, but a part of me was happy. Londo's little world was going to come crashing down now that his baby was dead. I knew he was going to try to seek revenge on Maceo for it, but not if I could help it. I planned to get Maceo back and away from that bitch, Saiyah. De'Maceo was mine.

"Maceo, can you find out when they will be doing the procedure?"

"Yeah. Are you good, Tee?"

"I'm good, Mace. God might not come when you want him, but he's always right on time."

He nodded his head and headed out of the room. I lay back in the bed and tried to see if what Maceo said was true. After five minutes of no reaction from the baby, I sighed in defeat because I knew in my heart that he was gone. I wanted to be sad, but guilt wouldn't allow me.

After this procedure was done and I healed, I would be back to do what I wanted to do in the beginning: get my fucking man.

Chapter 22

Mario

A month later . . .

"Erian, bring yo' ass out the bathroom and bring that test yo' slick ass tried to hide under the sink." Erian had me fucked up if she thought I was about to let her talk herself into an abortion. I had more than enough money to take care of her, my baby, and great grands. I was not about to play with her ass.

I heard the bathroom door open, and she threw the test at me before walking into the closet. Picking it up, I saw that shit said positive. I felt a smile gracing my face, but I knew in Erian's head that we were moving too fast. We forgot and forgave too fast. We had been rocking for this last month, but she had her own place, and I had my house.

Looking at the closet, I saw the light was off. How the hell was she going to find anything with the light off? Heading over there, I turned the knob, and it was locked. See, I knew her ass was on bullshit.

"Erian, you got to the count of five, and I'ma kick this bitch in."

She ain't answer.

"One . . . five!" I raised my foot and kicked that bitch in.

She looked at me and rolled her eyes.

"I don't give a fuck about yo' bald-head-ass rolling yo' mothafucking eyes, yo. What the fuck is the problem?"

"Really, Mario? What's my problem? We just got back together, and I'm pregnant already."

"And what the fuck is that supposed to mean? I thought you knew when you were fucking raw you could get pregnant. So what the fuck is you whining about now?"

She stopped and mugged me, but I glared right back at her ass. She lowkey sounded like she was saying she ain't want my seed.

"Mario, everything is moving too fast. I don't think we can have this baby." She whispered the last part.

"Nah, don't whisper now. Yo' ass was talking clear a second ago, so speak the fuck up."

"I said I don't think we can have this baby."

"I see," I said, leaning up against the door frame.

"You see? That's all you gotta say?"

"What the fuck yo' nappy, bald-head ass want me to say? You just told me you want to get rid of my seed. You see what that shit did to Maceo and Saiyah, right? That shit broke them, and if that's the route you wanna take, then so be it. But it won't be no coming back this time. Once I'm gone, I'm gone, and I mean that shit. Put that on my bitch-ass daddy's soul, whoever the nigga is."

She stood there staring at me for a minute before turning her back and getting ready for class. "Fucking selfish," I heard her mumble.

"How the fuck am I selfish? Because I want you to keep my fucking seed? If you were any other bitch, I would've made you abort it, but I'm fucking selfish. Fuck outta here, Erian. Get to school the best way you can."

I had to walk off on her ass. She knew I didn't strap up when we fucked. I never have, so her being mad about being pregnant was stupid as fuck, but I ain't have time to be entertaining her.

Leaving out the house, I saw a BMW parked in her parking spot. Walking toward it, I saw it was that punk-ass ex of hers. I tapped on the window. It rolled down, and he looked at me with a smirk.

"Fuck is you doing here?"

"Erian called me and said that we needed to talk. I assume it's about that positive pregnancy test she sent me."

I was seeing red. Hearing my name being called, I looked up at Erian, and she looked at the car. She was about to turn around.

"Bring yo' mothafucking ass here."

She turned around and slowly walked to me. I know she knew that was pissing me off.

"Yes, what's up?" she asked nonchalantly.

"You told this nigga you were pregnant by him? Is that why yo' ass hid in the bathroom and want the abortion?"

"Abortion? Erian, you ain't say shit about that. What the fuck is you trying to do? If you want the abortion, I'll pay for it. I don't need my wife finding out about this anyways."

I looked at Erian, and I could tell she didn't know he was married.

"Wi . . . wife? You're married? When? How? How long?"

"I've been married since I was twenty-one to my wife, Chantel. Being that I'm thirty-one, I'm sure you can do the math on how long I've been married."

Damn, this nigga played her good, but I wasn't going to say nothing.

"Wow! And I didn't send you that for you to have me tracked. I sent you that along with the message: 'Leave me the fuck alone.' I never told you I was pregnant by you with yo' minute-man ass. And we never even had sex like that. Had I known you had a wife, you wouldn't even be able to sample this. Bye, Roman."

"Minute man? Alright, gone head and front for your boy. With your no-dick-sucking ass."

I laughed at that one because he sounded like a pussy, and I knew that her ass could swallow a whole dick. Shit, she just did mine last night. And she had no gag reflexes.

"Fuck is so funny, lame, broke-ass nigga?"

I looked at that nigga and started laughing again. "Nigga, what? I don't fuck with you. I don't even know you, pussy, so fuck off my property. And I'm far from broke. You are driving a 2014 BMW. I'm driving a 2017 Maserati. Fuck nigga, up out my face before I knock yo' ass out," I barked.

I swear that pussy-ass nigga rolled his eyes.

I saw Maceo and Saiyah pulling up. The car stopped, and they both hopped out.

"What's up, Rio, Erian? What's going on?"

"Nothing. Bye, Roman," Saiyah and Erian said at the same time.

"Fuck you, bitch. I'm glad Drew had a hand in bringing you to yo' knees, stuck-up-ass bitch," he said to Saiyah.

How the fuck was this nigga finding out everything? Somebody was giving this nigga all the juice on us. Shit had me side-eyeing Erian.

"Aye, nigga, watch yo' mouth when you are talking about mine. Move around real quick, bro, because this def ain't want you want," Maceo snapped at that nigga.

I wasn't saying shit because I felt like Erian was up to some sneaky shit. Dude rolled the windows up, and he pulled off. I looked at Erian, and she looked scared.

"Take yo' dumb ass in the house. I'll catch y'all later."

I walked off behind her. Jogging up the stairs after her, I pushed her ass into the apartment.

"How the fuck does that nigga know all of our business?"

She looked around for a minute before looking at me. "Well, we were together still when everything went down.

I didn't know who to talk to, so I talked to my man at the time," she snapped.

"I don't give a fuck what you say about me or my brother, but yo' best fucking friend. You told her business to that nigga. Did you not see that girl fucking face? That's yo' fucking problem, Erian. You're irrational as fuck. You did that shit in the past, and you still doing it now. And how that fuck nigga knows where yo' head laying? I dare yo' ass to lie."

"He brought me home one day."

I had to make sure I heard her right. "Run that shit past me again."

"Oh my God! He brought me home one day. Damn, Mario."

I wanted to smack the fuck outta her. "Why the fuck would you bring a drug dealer to our fucking house?"

"What are you talking about? Roman owns a car lot, a grocery store, and a laundromat."

I wanted to smack her ass even more now. "Erian, you sound stupid as fuck. That nigga is a drug dealer. The lowest-on-the-totem-pole type of nigga."

"How the fuck do you know that?" she snapped, and I had to think about if I wanted to tell her.

"Because Maceo and I are the connect," I mumbled.

"You're what?"

"I'm the fucking connect. I never told you because I didn't want you to know. Hell, nobody knows."

"Wow! And you're talking about bringing a drug dealer to our house, but you're one."

"One, I ain't no drug dealer. I supply the niggas who are. And I don't corrupt nobody fucking life. The mothafuckas who chose to do drugs do so because they want to. Even if I didn't flood the fucking streets with the shit, somebody would. What Maceo and I got going on is a no-face, no-case type of shit. Only two people have ever seen our faces, and I plan to keep it that way."

"Who are those people?"

"I can't tell you that. If it ever came time for some shit to go down, I don't want you to know shit."

She nodded her head, and I pulled her to me. "Look, I ain't trying to get you caught up in my lifestyle. I've kept it a secret for the last ten years, and I plan to keep it that way. Mace hasn't told Saiyah, and I don't know if he will. Just relax and let me handle shit while you in school. But the abortion you are thinking about, you can dead that shit now. I already lost one child. I'm not willing to lose another."

"I don't know if I can do it, Mario. I'm still not over it."

"Think about what you are saying. You're willing to allow them to take something that God gave us a second chance with. Don't kill my seed, Erian."

I wasn't a begging-ass nigga, but for my seeds, I'd beg until I died, especially if they were by Erian. Now, I know y'all looking at me sideways, so let me explain. I would take care of all my seeds. It didn't matter who they were by, but I wouldn't be begging some random bitch that I fucked to keep my child. I wanted my children to all have the same mother, and I could see Erian being the one.

Seeing Maceo propose, I knew I wasn't ready for that step just yet, but he and Saiyah had something more than Erian and I. They connected on different levels than we did, and I understood that.

"Mario, I don't want you to regret moving so fast."

"We not really moving too fast. We are just learning each other again. Not much has changed, but still, we are learning together. Just think about what I'm saying."

She nodded her head. "Okay, Mario. I'll think about it. What's your name in the streets, so if I hear something, I can tell you?"

"The Reed brothers."

"Why Reed? Your last name is Perkins."

"Actually, it's Reed-Perkins."

"Well, damn. I've been hearing y'all name for the longest and didn't know it was y'all. It's a small world, I tell ya. Well, I done missed my one class for today, so I'ma go ahead and climb in the bed."

"Shit, say no more. I'm about to come lay up under you for the rest of the day."

"Come on then, daddy."

She took her clothes off and crawled into bed, and I followed behind her. For the rest of the day, I laid up under her, watching TV and making plans.

Chapter 23

Saiyah

Erian was dragging me to Maceo and Mario's studio grand opening. I didn't want to go, but I had been back home for a while, and she was trying to get me to go out. I didn't have anybody to watch Macayla, but she told me that her mother would watch her along with Li'l Maceo. I didn't know if I wanted her to go over there, but then Ms. Erin agreed to come watch them at the house. I was ever so grateful, especially since the incident with Drew. Maceo had cameras, so I would be able to watch them.

I was putting my lipstick on when I heard Erian's ghetto ass outside, blowing the horn. I didn't understand why she had to come to a quiet neighborhood and do that mess. All these white folks, and she wanted to make all this noise.

Hurrying up and grabbing my jacket as I headed out the front door, I saw her sitting in her BMW i8. Admiring it, I opened the door and got in.

"Bihhh, I see Mario got you riding pretty. Why would he give your pregnant ass this fast car?"

"Girl, I had to give this nigga some head to get this car. And I must say, it was well worth it," she said, wiping the corner of her lips.

"You a mess. But where is this studio at?"

"Downtown on Michigan Ave, the busiest fucking street in Chicago. Why, Lord, why did he have to pick down there?"

"Because like you said, it's one of the busiest streets," I said to her as I sat back in the seat and enjoyed the ride.

"So, how you are feeling, boo?" she asked me.

"Honestly, I feel better. I appreciate Maceo for everything that he did, that y'all did. I know I said some hurtful shit to you, Erian, and I apologize for that."

"Stop apologizing, Saiyah. You weren't in your right mind, and it's understandable, but the next time some shit like that happens and you don't tell me, we're going to have a fucking problem."

"I understand, and I'm sorry for not telling you. I just didn't know what to do."

"If I were you, I would've done the same thing, but you know you can always come to me, and I mean always. I love you, Yah," she said as she looked over at me and we pulled up to a red light.

"I love you too, hoe. Don't get all sentimental on me," I said, dabbing the corner of my eyes.

"Hey, hoe! I see you looking cute tonight," she said to me.

I laughed at her because she swore the only thing I ever wore were jeans and jogging pants.

"You think Mace's baby mama gon' show up?" she asked, and I rolled my eyes.

"Maceo told me that story she told him, and I don't believe half the shit that bitch said. Something about that bitch rubs me the wrong way. I promise if that bitch gets outta pocket, I'm straight dragging that bitch. I put that on everything I love."

"Yeah, Mario told me that shit, and I didn't believe more than two sentences from her mouth. She just trying to use Maceo, but that nigga cut that ass off. I laughed when Mario told me what they did."

I nodded my head, and the car grew silent. I couldn't believe that bitch wasn't using money for their son. Instead, she was buying shit for her and that bum-ass nigga.

The car came to a stop, and I looked around. It was a long-ass line to get inside, and mothafuckas was really waiting. As we got out, she fixed her clothes, then locked her door. She handed the keys to valet before we headed toward the door.

"Benji, what's up, cuz? I ain't seen yo' ass in a minute," Erian said.

"Oh, shit, Ms. Mayweather in the building. What are you doing here, cuz?"

"This my nigga's and his brother's grand opening. My name at the top of yo' list."

He scanned the list and nodded his head. "You and Saiyah?" he asked curiously.

"That would be me. And I can't believe yo' ass don't remember me, Benji."

He looked at me before putting his hand to his mouth. "Hell, nah. Not li'l miss Saiyah. What's up, girl?" he asked me, pulling me into a hug.

"Benji, if you want yo' job, bro, you'll back up off my old lady. Real shit, nigga," I heard Maceo say.

Turning around, I had to stop myself from jumping on him. This nigga was Versace'd down, then had the nerve to not be wearing a shirt underneath the suit jacket he had on.

"Damn, bae. That ass sitting up nice in that dress," he said, pulling me into a kiss.

I wrapped my arms around him and returned the gesture.

"Damn, Sai, you are messing with the boss now. My bad, bro," he said to Mace, and we headed inside.

Erian and Mario looked to be having a heated discussion. I winked at Benji, and he smiled. Entering the studio, I noticed that it wasn't just a studio, but it was a club along with it. The DJ had the music going, and everything was going good as we headed up to the VIP. Sitting on the couches, I peeped a couple people I ain't know, but Mace obviously knew who they were for them to be in his section, so I relaxed.

Erian and Mario showed up about ten minutes later, and the DJ was playing Young Dolph's "Play Wit' Yo' Bitch." I stood up with Erian as we rapped it. The guys in the section were looking at us as we rapped it.

"Erian, sit yo' ass down. You are drawing attention with that little-ass dress that you got on."

She flipped him off, and he laughed at her.

I smiled as we all kicked back and enjoyed the scenery, until Maceo's loud-mouth-ass baby mama saw him and decided to Bogart her fucking way into the VIP.

"Uh, Maceo. I know you seen me calling you. Why the fuck you got this mixed-breed-ass bitch up here, but I couldn't get in here?"

"Look, bitch, I'm not going to be too many more bitches. The next time you step outta line, you ain't gotta worry about Maceo saying shit because I'ma smooth tap that ass, fucking crackhead."

"I'ma crackhead, but our baby daddy love hitting this crackhead pussy like he did the other night."

I looked at Maceo, and he just sat there, stoic. That led me to believe one of two things: he did fuck her, or he was just trying to hold his composure. I was about to find out, though.

"Oh, yeah, he's your baby daddy, but my man and fiancé. So y'all fucked. Where the proof at?"

"All the proof I need is that you called him, and he hit that ignore button. He was too busy, knee deep in this tight pussy."

I looked back at a Maceo, and he dropped his head.

The music was loud, so you had to be within proximity of us to hear what she said. Luckily, I was the only one who heard it.

"What you gotta say about what she said, Maceo?"

He looked at me, pleading not to do it on his night, but fuck that. This nigga wanted to be with her, then so be it.

"You really think he wanted you and that ugly-ass little girl?"

Before I knew it, I had hauled off and punched that bitch dead in her face. She could say whatever she wanted about me, but Macayla Santaria Perkins, she could never put her mouth on my daughter.

"Bitch, don't you ever in yo' mothafucking life have my daughter name in yo' mouth, you rat-mouth-ass bitch."

I turned to walk away, and she grabbed my hair and pulled, almost making me lose my footing. I gained it quickly and flipped around on her. Hitting her in the head, I caught her off guard because I knew that she couldn't fight. By pulling my hair, she thought she was going to have leverage over me. Boy, was she wrong.

After I had flipped around on her, I started throwing blows to her face. I knew that shit hurt because my hand was hurting, but I didn't give a fuck. Each hit hurt worse than the first time.

Letting my hair go, she stumbled back, but she grabbed my hair, yanking me down to the ground before I got leverage over her and sat on her and hit that bitch all in her face. She yelled for Maceo to help, but instead, he lit his blunt and watched. After a couple of seconds, he came and pulled me off her, whispering something in my ear. I calmed down for a little bit but pushed him off me and stormed down the stairs. Mace and that bitch both had me fucked up.

"Get the fuck outta my shit, Tee," he said to her as I vanished down the stairs.

I headed down to the studio area that he showed me and tried to calm down. That nigga had me fucked up. That nigga swore that she wasn't going to be an issue, but I knew that was a fucking lie. She wanted Maceo, and I wasn't about to fight that bitch over him. They could have each other as far as I was concerned.

The door to the studio opened, and Maceo stood there, staring at me.

Chapter 24

Teriana

Getting up from the floor was a task within itself. I couldn't feel my face nor my body. Getting outside to my car, I called the police. She must've been stupid if she thought I was gon' let her get away with that.

"Chicago Police Department, how may I assist you?"

"Yes, my baby father has just beaten me up. I can hardly see out of my left eye. Oh my God! I think he's coming for me." I banged on the window.

"Leave me alone, De'Maceo. Get the fuck away from me. Help! He's got a gun, and he's threatening me." I rattled off the address, and I heard her typing.

"Miss, please don't open the door. The police are en route to you."

"Please. I'm scared for my life," I cried, then banged on the window again.

"I'm on the phone with the police, and they will be here soon. Leave me alone." I banged on the window, then breathed a fake sigh of relief. I should be an actor by the way I was putting on a performance for them. Maceo was going to wish he had helped me.

Fuck Maceo and that bitch. He came through the other day to get Li'l Mace, and I gave him some bomb-ass head. I tried to ride that nigga dick, but he wasn't with that. So, since he wouldn't give me the dick and admit to his li'l fiancée that we almost fucked, I was going to make his life a living hell.

De'Maceo Santana Perkins belonged to me, and the sooner he learned that, then we wouldn't have a fucking problem.

"Miss, are you still there? Police are on their way to your car. Is he still around?"

"Um, no, he isn't around. He ran off after I showed that I was on the phone with the police." I looked up, and the police were coming my way. "Oh, thank God, they are here. Thank you, Miss," I said, ending the call.

I got out of the car and ran over to the police. "He went back inside. He said that he would get me another time. Please, you must go inside and get him. He was upstairs in the VIP section. His name is De'Maceo Perkins. He owns the club."

"Miss, please calm down. We already have our men on it. Let's get you to the ambulance so we can check you out."

I followed behind the officer. The radio came through that they had Maceo. Trying to keep my game face on, I looked around, paranoid, as they walked him outta the club and proceeded to put him in the backseat. I looked at him, and he had a smirk on his face. I was enjoying every minute of this, but once that smirk disappeared from his face, he mouthed his threat loud and clear.

Turning my head, I pulled the blanket over me as Mario, his bitch, and that hoe Saiyah walked outta the club. They looked my way, and nobody said anything, but the smile on Saiyah's face spoke enough to let me know that she would be back for more.

"Miss, you'll have to come down to the station so that we can take pictures and you can file an official report."

I nodded my head and got into the ambulance with the assistance of the paramedics.

"Can I drive my own car to the station? I need to check on my son." I asked as I formulated the plan in my head.

"Yes, you can, but we need you to come directly down to the station. We don't want scum like that to walk the Earth," the fat, redneck officer said.

I nodded my head with a thank you and rushed toward my car. I watched the ambulance and the police pull off before I continued to my car. It was now in my line of vision, and I was near it, but a blow to the back of my head momentarily deterred my plans.

"I see you think this is a fucking joke. You didn't really think I was going to let you get away. I'ma give you two options. You can go down to the station and tell them what happened, or I'll make your life a living hell. You're a rat, and all rats must die. Just know your time is limited. Tick tock," she said, walking away, laughing.

Getting up, I ran toward my car and pulled away toward my house. It took me a while to get there, but once I did, I ran into the house, grabbed a couple of outfits, three rolls of money from the safe, and got the hell outta dodge.

The threat that Maceo made was loud and clear, but the one Saiyah stated expressed more passion and truth than Maceo's. Maceo always threatened to do something to me but never followed through. Li'l Mace would be safer with them than me because once Londo noticed I just took about 20K of his re-up money, I would be dead as hell.

As I looked at Chicago in my rearview mirror, I knew my decision to leave was for the best.

Chapter 25

Maceo

After Tee's ass limped outta here, I got up to go find Saiyah. I knew she was going to be pissed because I allowed Tee to give me some head, but that shit was unexpected, and it wasn't my intention to be on that with Tee, especially since I wanted to marry Saiyah. I wasn't even trying to be on that bullshit. I ain't never cheated on Saiyah, so I knew she was looking at me sideways. I had to go explain that shit to her.

We named the club Studio, but it had four studios inside, along with a club in the middle. The club only opened on Fridays and special occasions. Staring at her in the studio, I knew Saiyah was mad as fuck at me. Before I could even utter a word, she pushed me back.

"Really, Maceo, you really were fucking that bitch? Like, what the fuck was your purpose of proposing?" she snapped at me.

"Yah, calm down. I didn't fuck that girl. I mean, she did give me some head, but I ain't even nut. I swear, I wasn't on that with her," I said, then I realized how stupid I sounded.

"Really, do you know how fucking stupid you sound? You got head, but you ain't nut. Really, do I not give you enough pussy? Like, is her head better than mine? I mean, what could lead you to blatantly disrespect me and our engagement? Like, I don't even think we should be getting married if you can't keep yo' dick in yo' pants. Like, what the fuck, man?" She looked at me and wiped her tears, and I went to grab her, but she backed up.

"Don't touch me, Mace. Go enjoy the rest of your night, and I'll be out there shortly."

"Yah, don't do me like that, bae. I'm sorry. I fucked up. I just went to grab Li'l Mace, and one thing led to another. She tried to fuck, but I ain't have no rubbers . . ." I trailed off, and I realized I had just fucked up.

Saiyah looked at me and stormed out.

"Fuck!" I yelled out as I swiped shit off my desk. I couldn't fucking believe this shit. I wished I could kill that bitch for the shit that she pulled. That ass whooping was well deserved. When I found her, I was going to kill that bitch. Yeah, it was my fuck-up for even sitting down and talking to her, but I damn sure ain't expect her to give me no head or try to fuck.

Running out behind her, I made it back to the VIP section but was greeted by the police. I mugged the fuck outta them because I ain't fuck with none of them. Getting up the stairs, I saw Saiyah was sitting down, mugging me as I walked into the area.

"De'Maceo Perkins?" the white redneck officer asked me.

"Yeah, that's me. What y'all want with me?" I griped.

"You're under arrest for the assault and battery against Teriana Holt. You have the right to remain silent. Anything you say can and will be used against you in a court of law. You have the right to an attorney. If you can't afford one, one will be appointed to you."

I couldn't believe Tee's stupid ass called the police on me, but I had something for that bitch. She thought she was going to get away with it, but it was going to be something she least expected.

"Wait! Hol' up. My fiancé didn't do that. I was the—"

I shook my head at Saiyah. She looked at me pleading, but I wouldn't let her.

"Rio, let Zan run the club, bro. Come bail me out. Saiyah, go home."

The police yanked on me, and I was walked out the door. I wasn't about to resist and have them beat my ass, or worse, kill me. I ain't with the shit they be on.

Saiyah was just about to take the charge for me, but I couldn't even let her do that. Call it trying to make up for Tee giving me head, or apologizing, but I refused to lose Saiyah again over some stupid-ass mistake that I had made. Walking out of the club, I saw the ambulance and police cars, but more importantly, I saw Tee looking at me. I smirked at the bitch before I let that bitch know I was coming for her. Saiyah wasn't going to worry about that bitch after this, because I was going to put her in the dirt. She should've took that ass whooping and kept it pushing.

As they drove me to the downtown station, I knew that I was going to be convicted for that shit because Tee wasn't no dummy. I bet her ass made it seem real, like I had really been attacking her. My ass wasn't about to sit in anybody's jail for shit I ain't do. I had cameras all through that club, and I know they caught Saiyah and me and that ass-whooping that Tee received, courtesy of Saiyah.

The police talked amongst themselves, but what caught my ears was that somebody was trying to snitch on Trouble and Murder Reed. If I wasn't pissed before, I was pissed now. Mothafuckas always wanted to snitch on some shit they didn't know.

All I had to do was make one phone call, and all this shit would disappear, but I wasn't trying to call Chyla unless it was necessary. The Cartel didn't play that, and if there was a snitch in the camp, she would find out before me.

While I had Chicago on lock since Angel left and moved to California, Chyla brought us in under the Cartel. The difference was that we were the plug. I didn't have to answer to anybody. The Cartel was more than drug dealers and kingpins. Just about everyone had a legit hustle. Chyla and her husband, Delgado, had been around since I was coming up. Their asses had me snatched off the street, brought to their headquarters, and offered me the deal. But you already know I had my own rules and didn't like answering to nobody. They agreed I operated on my own.

The whole thing seemed odd. That was, until I was told that my mother is her aunt and she had found out. Being that all her blood family was dead, we were the closest she had to it, so she had to help us.

At first, I wanted to say fuck that deal, but at the time, Mario was fighting a gun case that he was going to lose. I told her I would accept if she helped him and he could be my right hand. It took her all of thirty minutes to have the case dismissed. She let me have free reign, and I'd been balling ever since. I was nickel and diming from the ages 15 to 21, but when I met Saiyah, Chyla had me assemble my own team. Everyone thought I got outta the game, but really, all these niggas were eating because of me.

She caught me up on the basics, signs of loyalty and disloyalty. I had to admit she was gutta and thorough as fuck. No matter what, Chyla came through for a nigga, and I appreciated cuzzo for it. Each time I got a chance, I sent her a thank-you gift.

She was in Mexico with her husband and two kids. How she raised a family and ran the Cartel and Mafia together was like the President running the U.S., but I couldn't do that shit. My ass would be laid out.

Feeling the air hit my face, I saw the door was open, and they were dragging me out of the car. I ended up hitting the ground. A shadow came from out of the dark, and I just stared at it, not moving.

"Why on my first night home do I have to get yo' ass outta trouble?" the voice said, removing their hood. I already knew who it was.

"Uncuff him, and I expect for this incident to never have happened. Do we understand?"

The officers nodded their heads before the redneck one uncuffed me, and I walked over to her. They got in their squad car and got the fuck outta there.

"What's up, cuz? What brings you to the Chi?" I asked.

"I heard you killed the leaders of your team. What was the cause?"

"I treat all my people equally and with respect. Those li'l niggas were disrespectful as fuck. I don't tolerate the down-talking and thinking you above niggas. On top of that, those niggas allowed killers to walk away knowing they had my money and my drugs. You can't run shit and turn a blind eye to mothafuckas plotting on you. I refused to have anybody taking food from my kids' mouth over greed, when everybody is getting a decent cut out the deal."

She was quiet for a minute. "I definitely hear you, cuz, but I had to make this trip personally. I know you and Mario keeping it on the DL about y'all running drugs through the Chi, but I need you to put yo' girl up on game. She doesn't need to know about your do's and don'ts, but she needs to know what you do. Yo' ass kept her a secret from me, and I feel like I'm being robbed of friends," she said, smirking at me.

"You don't need no damn friends. What happened to Princess?"

"Princess is around somewhere. We aren't friends at this moment. She's going through something with the death of her husband still, and finding out he has another child outside of their son. It's been four years, and she's still grieving, but finding out he had another child broke her down. I don't know if we will ever be friends again, but I honestly wouldn't be affected. I have visited her and have security watching her."

Damn, Liam had been gone for a while, so she must've been taking it harder, knowing he fucked around on her and produced another seed.

"De'Maceo Santana?" Chyla called my name.

"My fault, cuz. What was you saying?"

"Dinner, tomorrow at eight. I expect you and Mario to be in attendance, along with your women and children. Oh, and for your information, your baby mother is fleeing, but I got eyes on her. A car is waiting for you at the end of the trail. Everything is handled. I got you, cuz. Remember what I said about dinner tomorrow. Have a good night."

I nodded my head, jogged to the car, and got inside.

Pulling into my driveway, I saw the lights on in our room go out, so I assumed Saiyah was going to bed. As I sat contemplating if I wanted to go inside, my phone rang. It was Saiyah calling. Hitting the ignore button, I thanked the driver before going in and facing the music.

When I entered our bedroom, Saiyah was lying on her side. Going in the bathroom, I stripped outta my clothes, I turned on the shower and got in. With my head under the water, I tried to wash the day off, but that all went out the window when I felt the cool air flowing into the shower.

Saiyah wrapped her arms around my waist, and I relaxed.

"Mace, what's going on? What did they say? How did you get here? We checked the police station, and nothing."

"Yah, I gotta tell you something, but I need to know that you're going to still be with me regardless."

"I'll never tell you that. Let me choose how I feel about it before you throw that ultimatum, De'Maceo."

Nodding my head as I held it under the water, I didn't know what to say. If I told her this shit, it may add to the bullshit with Tee, and I was not even with that shit, but before she met Chyla, she needed to know.

"I'm the plug," I quickly said.

Her arms dropped from around my waist. "You're the what?"

"I'm the plug. In the streets, you hear Trouble Reed. That's me. I've been selling drugs since I met you. I know you thought I quit, but I didn't. I wanted to tell you all the time that I was messing with you, and everyone believes that I quit selling years ago, but really, I'm the plug and the reason so many drugs is flooding the streets."

"Maceo, tell me that you're lying."

I heard the choking in her voice. Turning around, I pulled her to me.

"Yah, I can't tell you that. I love you, ma, and I needed to tell you. I can't tell you my do's and don'ts. Sometimes, I'll get calls calling me outta the bed late at night. Sometimes, I must make trips to places. Ma, with this comes a lot of responsibility, but I do it, bae. I can just tell you who I am so you're aware. You haven't even known that you have a full security detail following you. You're protected, ma. I hope you believe me when I say I would never let anything happen to you, nor my kids."

"Maceo, I want us to be honest. Why didn't you tell me back then? I would've been on your side regardless. I've heard you and Mario's name for the longest. Yes, I know Mario is really Trouble and you're Murder. You have the potential to be cold-blooded and a killer, and I've seen the murder in your eyes before, baby. I can't believe that you hid this for so long."

"You don't care about what I do, do you?"

"Maceo, why would I? You take care of me and your kids like no other, baby. I want you to love me, and you have. The incident with Tee, I'm going to let fly because she got yo' ass by calling the police. But let's be clear. The next bitch you stick your dick in, I don't care if it's her mouth or pussy, we are over. I will not tolerate a nigga cheating on me. I love you, but I love me more, bae."

I nodded my head as we stood underneath the water. Saiyah had her real hair in, so I ran my fingers through it and down her body. She had nothing on, and my dick was getting harder. Dropping to her knees, she blessed me with the best nut a nigga could get off. After we got out of the shower, my head hit the pillow, and I was out like a light.

Chapter 26

Erian

Standing at the door and knocking, I had on my trench coat with my birthday suit underneath. Hearing the doors unlock, I struck a pose, showing a li'l leg action. The door swung open, and there stood my man in all his chocolate glory.

I had to make sure I pulled this li'l session off, especially after the argument tonight. My insecurity was kicking in, and I didn't want to blame the pregnancy, but I swear my emotions were at an all-time high.

"Damn, how may I help you, Miss?"

"Yeah, I'm looking for De'Marrion Perkins. Um . . . I was sent here as a gift for him."

"Oh, yeah, who sent this gift? I need to send them a special thank you," he said, running his tongue across his bottom lip.

"His wife did," I said, looking at him underneath my bangs.

"My wife? Well, she must've wanted me to wrap this gift if she sent it to me. Come on inside," he said, yanking me in the house and closing the door.

Slowly dropping the coat, I revealed that I had nothing on underneath it. He turned around and looked at me before licking his lips.

"Got damn! Spin around me for me, baby girl."

I did as he was told. Walking over to me, he pushed me down until I was on my knees in front of him. Quickly unbuckling his belt and pulling his pants down, I came face to face with my other best friend.

Wrapping my hand around it, I worked my hand slowly up and down. He had his eyes closed. Leaning forward, I wrapped my lips around the shaft, slowly teasing him. Tired of teasing him, I took him all the way in my mouth. Hearing him letting out a string of obscenities, I continued to swallow him whole.

"Fuck, Eri! Suck this dick just like daddy taught you," he said, wrapping his hands up in my hair, slowly fucking my mouth.

"Mmmmm!" I moaned out.

Reaching between my legs, I played with my pussy as I gave him some head. It was turning me on, all the faces that he was making.

I guess he realized that I was playing with my pussy because he pulled outta my mouth. "Get on the couch and spread them legs," he told me.

Getting up, I hurried to the couch and got in the position that he liked me in. Kneeling in front of me, he slipped two fingers inside of me before his tongue separated my pussy lips and he went to work. I couldn't contain the moans and yelps that were coming from my mouth because that's how good he was.

My legs started shaking, and he used his hands to open my lips up wider before pulling my clitoris in his mouth and sucking on it. Letting my legs go, I pulled his head in deeper as I felt my eyes roll into the back of my head.

"Hold them legs up," he said, slapping me on the ass.

"Mmmmmm, fuck, Mario!" I yelled out as I went back to holding my legs. His fingers and tongue were doing the magic.

"Fuck that! What's my name?" he asked, removing his mouth, and I got mad.

"I'm sorry, papi. Please finish," I moaned out as he went back to sucking and licking all on my fat pussy.

"Cum all on daddy's tongue for him," he said, pushing my legs further back and sticking his face all in it.

I couldn't move if I wanted to. That's how good it was, and I felt the orgasm working its way through my body. "Papi, I'm about to cum," I yelled out as I came all over his tongue.

He licked up every drop.

"Mmmmmm!" I moaned as he continued to lick and suck on my clit.

"Damn, your shit sweet," he said, standing up, rubbing the head of his dick between my lips.

I couldn't contain the moan that came out. Reaching between us, I guided him into his favorite spot.

"Damn, girl! Yo' shit tight," he said, slowly moving in and out of me.

I snapped my eyes shut and reveled in the feeling of him.

"No, open them eyes and watch," he told me as he pulled me to the end of the couch and started driving deeper into me.

I couldn't breathe from how deep he was. "Oh my God! Slow down, Mario."

"Naw, yo' ass came over here teasing me, so shut up and take this dick," he told me, pulling out and tapping me to flip over. Without warning, he slipped right into me. Grabbing my hair, he pulled me to him.

"You see what the fuck you caused?" he said, and I nodded my head. "Throw that shit back then," he told me.

Matching his speed, I tightened around him.

"Fuck!" he yelled out as he smacked my ass cheeks. "Yo' ass playing dirty," he said, pulling out of me and falling on the couch.

Breathlessly turning over, I saw that he was still standing tall. Hurrying up, I climbed over to him and eased down in his lap. Putting my hands above my head, I showed him no hands. Lifting and dropping down on him, I rode his dick like I was trying to win a prize.

He put his hands on my hips, plowing into me from the bottom, and that shit felt so good.

"Get that shit, bae," he said, slapping me on the ass.

Doing my signature move, I bounced my ass cheeks up and down on his dick while I twerked a li'l bit. His head fell back against the couch, and his eyes rolled into the back of his head. I felt his body shiver a li'l bit before he reached between us and started playing with my pearl. My head fell back as I placed my hands on his chest to ride him.

"Catch this wave, bae," he said as I came on his stomach and he came in me.

"Fuckkkkk, Eri!" he yelled out.

I laid my forehead against his.

"I can't be fucking around with you, man. Gon' give a nigga a heart attack," he said, and I laughed, kissing him on his lips.

"Don't get shit started knowing that you can't finish it," he told me.

Climbing off him, I bent over in front of him and used his cum as a lubricant to play with my clit.

"Say what now?" I asked him.

"Make that ass clap," he said, and I did just that.

"Damn, girl! Let's get this round two popping in the shower," he said.

I straightened up and followed behind him.

Later that evening, Mario and Mace told Saiyah and me that we had a dinner to go to. Li'l Mace and Macayla were with us. I didn't know what type of dinner we were going to at someone's house, but I was going to relax and enjoy myself.

Pulling up to the house, I looked over at Saiyah, but she didn't look surprised. Side-eyeing her for the moment, I looked ahead as the guards motioned for them to move through the gates that had the letters *CM* on them.

In front of the house, I saw a woman and man standing outside. Mace stopped the truck and got out as our doors were opened by security that I didn't even see before. Stepping out of the truck with their assistance, I walked over to Mario. He wrapped his arms around me as we followed the man and woman into the house.

I swear this was some shit off *MTV Cribs*. A waterfall with fish at the bottom was in the center of the foyer. Looking around, I saw they had expensive furniture and these high-ass ceilings. I just know this house cost them some bread because this shit was too damn nice.

We finally made it to the dining room, and another man and woman were sitting at the table with two children.

"De'Marrion, De'Maceo, it's nice of you to join us. Who are these two lovely ladies and this handsome guy and gorgeous lady?"

"Chyla, this is my girl, Erian. She my baby mama, too," he said, rubbing my stomach.

"Hi, Erian. I'm Chyla Wilson, owner and CEO of the Davenport Cartel," she said with a smile on her face.

Never letting my emotions show, I smiled back at her.

"And I'm Saiyah Brady—well, soon to be Saiyah Perkins. I'm De'Maceo's fiancée. This is Macayla and T'Maceo. They are Maceo's children."

"I like you already. I assume De'Maceo has told you about me. Erian seems lost. Mario, you didn't," she said, looking at me.

"Didn't what?" I asked.

"Mommy, is it alright if we go to the playroom?"

"Yes, DJ."

All the kids ran behind him.

"Why, Mario?" she asked him.

He shrugged his shoulders.

"Well, let's eat. The children will eat in the playroom."

"I'm not eating until Mario explains why I'm not aware of you."

"Erian, I don't wanna talk about it."

"Can y'all excuse us?" I pulled Mario back out of the dining room and into the foyer.

"What's going on? Why didn't I know who she was? Are you fucking her?"

He looked at me before laughing. "Am I fucking my cousin? Nah, that's some incestuous shit right there. Besides, I wanted you to believe that she was somebody I used to fuck. This is payback for that nigga Roman knowing where you lived. Come on. Chyla is my mom's sister's daughter. She's my first cousin. And I would never have you in the presence of a bitch I fucked," he said, then we made our way back into the dining room.

Everyone was sitting around talking.

"Glad you could return. I'm Chyla, their cousin, and this is my husband, Delgado. I didn't want to make you uncomfortable, so I told them to tell y'all about me. I see Mario's childish ass didn't," she said, laughing.

"Fuck you, Chy, straight up," he said, fixing our plates.

"Aye, have y'all heard from Angel?" Maceo asked.

"Yeah, him and AJ were just up here recently. That nigga got remarried, and his wife is pregnant with their daughter."

"Word. I pray I'm having a little girl," Mario said, and the whole table looked at him.

"Hell, nah. You don't want that shit, bruh. I'm telling you. For Desi, I have three guards wherever she is at. I don't give a fuck. My baby girl is pretty as fuck, and I'm liable to kill every nigga that look her way." Then, a string of Spanish words flew from his mouth.

"Babe, calm down. Why the fuck you bring up a daughter? Damn!" Chyla snapped.

I laughed at them, along with Saiyah. I started eating my food as the talk circulated around the room until the kids ran toward us, letting us know some man was outside their window. Hearing glass break, Chyla, Delgado, Maceo, and Mario pulled their guns out.

"DJ, take Desi and the kids to your room and get in your closet. Don't come out until I get you," Delgado said. His son grabbed the kids' hands and ran up the stairs.

"Boss, we have the perp. We don't know how he got in, but he seemed to have been staring at the little girl that came to visit. He's in the playroom with Brash. Come and look," one of the guards said.

"Memphis, what the fuck? How did the window even get broke?"

"Sorry, boss. I'll replace it, but I smashed his head through it."

Delgado nodded his head, and we followed behind him.

"What the fuck? Demarcius, what the fuck are you doing in my house? How did you get out?" Chyla snapped.

I looked at everyone else, and they were confused.

"What the fuck you mean how I got out? Look what I'm wearing. How do you think I got out?" the man asked her.

"Babe, who is this man?" Delgado asked Chyla as he pulled her close.

"He's De'Maceo and De'Marrion's father."

"What?" they yelled.

"I'm sorry, y'all. I found out that y'all father was in jail and had no idea about y'all. Although y'all are nine months apart, he had no idea that either of you was born. Now, back to you. Why the fuck are you staring at

Maceo's daughter? I hope you not on some pedophile shit, Demarcius. I would hate to kill you," Chyla threatened.

Everyone got quiet because you could hear the ice dripping from her voice

"I don't like no fucking kids. Don't play me like that, Chyla. She looked so much like Maceo's mother and your mom. It was hard not to stare at her. But I ain't no damn pedophile. Never have been, never will be. Don't disrespect me like that again."

Chyla stepped closer to him and looked in his face. "No, you don't fucking disrespect me. You came to my fucking house, looking at my babies. I don't give a fuck who you are. I will have you killed where you stand and have no remorse. I know you checked out who I was, so don't let this hair, these nails, and this expensive outfit fool you. I will body you and then fuck my nigga until he's in a coma. Next time, use the front fucking door. Do you understand?"

He looked at her and nodded his head. I couldn't believe these grown-ass men were afraid of her, but then again, I saw why.

"Yo, Chyla? What the fuck, man? Why did you look for this nigga?" Mario snapped, but I could see that it was hitting him hard. He had unshed tears in his eyes.

I went over to him and attempted to pull him out of the room.

"I'm not leaving without my brother," Mario said.

Mace looked at him and nodded his head. "Aye, bro, can you go get my kids, man? I'm ready to go," Maceo stated.

"Wait a fucking minute! De'Marrion Constantine Reed-Perkins and De'Maceo Santana Reed-Perkins, get y'all mothafuckin' ass back in the dining room and have a seat. You will not do this, sir. Not under my watch," Chyla said.

Her husband just stood off in the corner, watching everything going on.

"I don't want to sit at the table with this fuck nigga, man," Mario snapped harshly.

"Li'l nigga, who the fuck is you disrespecting? She just told y'all punk asses that I didn't know about y'all. Yo' crackhead-ass mama is the reason I was where I was in the first fucking place. I had to kill that nigga she fucking stole bricks from. I'm not talking one or two. Yo' mama stole ten of that man's bricks. You know how much money he lost, and yo' mama put the fucking blame on me. When I see her, the bitch gon' wish I had killed her instead."

"Yo don't disrespect my fucking mama, nigga. She might not have been shit, but she was all we had."

I looked at Mario, and he was in a fighting stance.

"Bro, chill out. I wanna hear what the old head gotta say. Who was the nigga my mama took bricks from, and how she get that close to 'em?" Maceo spoke.

"I didn't know yo' mama was even on that shit. I was traveling from state to state, doing shit. I had my own business and dealings on the side. Yo' mama wasn't aware of those side dealings, and I didn't even know she was even pregnant. I had several women, but your mother was one of the mains. De'Maceo, I had no clue that your mother had you. I still didn't know about you. Your mother gave you to a sitter and paid her to keep you. De'Marrion, your mother told me she had aborted you. I never knew that you were even born, son. Your mother is a mass manipulator.

"Do y'all think I would've let y'all sleep on streets and struggle like y'all did? I have money that sets you, my grandkids, great grandkids, and my great-great-grandkids up. I would've never fucked y'all over. I love y'all. Even if I don't know y'all that well, I wouldn't do shit to harm y'all nor my grandkids."

"When you found out about us?" Mario asked, looking at him.

Delgado had long excused himself from the room.

"He found out a few weeks ago when I went to visit him. He honestly didn't know about y'all. I had to get a DNA test to prove y'all were his. Your mother told me who he was," Chyla said.

"You talked to that bitch. Where is she at?" Maceo asked.

"She's in detox, y'all. Your mother is my aunt, and as much as y'all hate her, she's family, and I don't kill family unless they leave me no choice. She went to rehab willingly, and I helped her. She has a long road to go, so until y'all are ready to see her, she will stay invisible."

"I don't have shit to say to her. That bitch sold me when I was seven to a fucking pimp. Nah, hell nah. Where she at, Chyla?"

"She did what?" Chyla asked.

I knew the story, and I also knew that the dude who did it molested Mario. He had never told Maceo.

"She sold me to a fucking pimp and that nigga . . . that nigga raped me. I can feel that nigga hands on the back of my neck." Mario broke down crying.

Maceo looked at Mario, and I looked at Saiyah, and she was crying. Maceo walked over to his brother and pulled him into a hug. He was saying something in his ear, but I couldn't hear it. Their daddy was standing in the corner, facing the wall.

"You mean to fucking tell me that bitch sold you to that bitch-ass pimp that she was fucking? Yo, I don't give a fuck about that bitch, Chyla. I want that hoe delivered to me now. I swear to God, you better get me that bitch ASAP."

I listened and watched him as he walked over to them. I couldn't believe their daddy was here, and this was what everything was coming down to. Chyla stepped out of the room and came back minutes later.

"I don't want to interrupt y'all, but it seems that we are going to have a problem. Your mother left the rehab and hasn't returned. I'll have the whole city searched for her. I told y'all earlier, I don't kill family, but for you, De'Marrion, if you want her dead, it can be handled."

"I want that bitch found and delivered to me. I don't care if she's sucking the devil's dick. Get me that bitch, Chy," Demarcius snapped.

"Consider it done. Erian, I know you are pregnant and hungry, so your food has been packaged, and you guys can leave, if you would like. This isn't how I expected our meeting, so if you ladies would be willing, I was having a spa day tomorrow and would love for you ladies to join me," Chyla said to Saiyah and me.

"We would love to. Just let the guys know, and we will be ready."

"I'll just text you ladies when the car arrives to each of you. Have a good night. Maceo and Mario, I love you guys, and you know I would go to war for y'all. Go home, get some rest for the next week or so, because the convention is coming up soon, and I need you guys in attendance."

"Alright, cuz. I got you," Maceo said, wrapping his arm around his brother's shoulder and walking him out of the house.

Saiyah and I followed behind him as the kids descended the stairs. Grabbing their hands, we all walked out of the house and got into the car.

This night started off great but ended badly. I knew more was to come when we got home. Mario had revealed his biggest secret, and I just prayed that everything went in his favor. I knew how much he wanted his dad and loved his mama, but it was time for him to let her go. Hopefully, their daddy could make her disappear forever.

Chapter 27

Maceo

It had been a couple of days since I learned about what happened to Mario, and no lie, that shit was eating me up on the inside. I couldn't do shit but cry when I heard that leave my brother's mouth. The fact that he kept it away from me so long and broke down at the sight of our pops made me feel like less than a man. I had been having a fucked-up attitude toward everybody, but mostly Saiyah. She was taking the brunt end of it, and she ain't deserve that shit. She ain't do shit to me, and I felt fucked up just thinking about how I treated her, but I didn't even know how to feel now.

My brother, my nigga since forever, just told me that some fucking pimp molested him and my mother knew. Seven, my brother was fucking seven. Macayla would be seven in a year, and I would be damned if anybody laid a hand on her. I would body anyone who attempted to bring harm to her. And Li'l Mace was three. If I ever found out some shit like that happened, I think I would have Chicago painted red for my kids. I loved the fuck outta my kids, and hearing my brother, my baby brother at that, tell me he was molested and I wasn't there to help him had stirred some shit up inside of me. I couldn't even look him in the eyes. And it wasn't because a nigga raped him, but because I failed him. If I could go back in time, I would stop her from taking him, but how could I do anything when she used to sell me for crack then buy me back after a week?

"Mace, your food is on the bed. The kids and I are going to the mall. Do you need anything else?"

I looked up at Saiyah as she looked at me, and I felt fucked up. Here she was making sure I was good, and I was treating her like shit. I wished I could reverse all that shit I said to her. Pulling her to me, I sat her in my lap.

"What is it, Maceo?"

"I wanted to apologize for how I've been treating you. It wasn't right. Just knowing what I know makes me feel like a fucked-up older brother. I'm supposed to protect Mario, and I couldn't and I didn't. What am I supposed to do?"

"There ain't nun you can do, bro. I've dealt with that. It's nothing for you to dwell on. Clearly, it had no effect on who I am and how I lived my life. You were eight, bro. How much could you have really done? Mama ain't no saint, and I don't care if the bitch lives or dies. I love her, but she was the worst parent we could've had, so get yo' ass up, and let's go see what this bitch gotta say. I love you, bro," Mario said, walking over to me from the doorway.

Saiyah got up and moved out the way as I stood up and pulled my brother into a hug.

"Why the fuck didn't you tell me, Mario? Why you keep that shit from me?" I asked him as tears escaped my eyes.

"Bro, wasn't shit that we could've done. Mama is the cause of all of this, man. I promise you, I would've told you if I thought you needed to know. I don't want you to dwell on it. Let it go for me, but most importantly, for yourself. I know you hurting and wish you could've saved me, but bro, I'm good. I love you, and you've been there every time I needed you. Missing that one doesn't mean shit to me."

I nodded my head. "I love you, too, man. Let me talk to Saiyah really quick."

He pulled out the hug and left the room.

I started to speak to Yah, but she stopped me.

"Don't apologize. I understand, Mace. If it was Erian, I would have felt the same way. Do you see how Erian treated me during the whole ordeal? You did what I did, and that's lash out. If no one understands that, I do. Your food is on the bed, your clothes are hanging up in the bathroom, and your water is ready. Go ahead and do what you need to do. The kids and I will see you when we return. Oh, and I enrolled in classes online. They start in August. Just thought I should let you know." She kissed my lips and left.

Sitting down on the bed, I grabbed the tray of food that my baby had made and devoured it. After I had finished my food, I soaked in the tub for an hour, then got out and got ready for the day.

About twenty-five minutes later, a knock came on my room door as I was tying my shoes. Telling the person to come in, I looked up and saw Mario.

"Congrats, bro!" he said, and I looked at him in confusion.

What the fuck is this nigga talking about? I thought.

"Bro, what you talm bout?"

He held up the pregnancy test that read positive, 2-3 months. I snatched that shit out of his hand and looked up at him. "Where you get this shit from?"

"The downstairs bathroom."

"What the fuck? She ain't even let me know she was carrying my seed?" I went to grab my phone but couldn't find it. "Fuck is my phone?"

"Bro, chill out. I don't even think she knows. She doesn't think she can have kids, remember? If she does know, give her a minute to let it register in her head. Let's worry about handling this situation with Pops and Ma, then you can worry about Yah."

I wanted to object, but I knew I needed to get this over with and give Yah her space.

Grabbing my keys and jogging down the stairs with Mario behind me, I left out the garage and set the alarm as I backed out.

I had a lot of love for my mama, but I also had a lot of hate for her. The shit she put us through wasn't worth it. I had to struggle to get my brother and me food, to get us clothed and into school. Hell, it took me years to graduate college. I just finished that shit a year ago, but I did it. I'd always been headstrong and determined, not letting anyone get me down, but knowing that my pops didn't know about me made me look at him differently. I guess I could give him a chance to be the father he always wanted to be. But one wrong move, and I would leave his ass stankin'. Pops or no pops, if a nigga crossed me wrong, I was deading him before he could dead me. These streets didn't love nobody. That's why, when I came home at night, all that street shit was left behind me once I crossed that threshold.

After the hour drive, we pulled up to the rehab gates. Giving them my name, I saw Chyla, her husband, and my pops all standing outside talking. Chyla had told me they found my mama in a crack house, but I didn't give a fuck. I made them detox her until she was coherent because I wanted her to answer every question that I had.

"What's up, y'all? Where she at?"

"That bitch down there fucking lying," my pops snapped, and Mario chuckled.

"Take me to her."

My pops led the way to her, and I was impressed by what they called a rehab. This shit was nice as fuck.

Getting to the door, Chyla pushed it open, and we walked in. In the corner sat a frail woman who rocked back and forth. I could tell we were going to be down here for a while.

"Ma!"

She looked at me, and her eyes lit up. "De'Maceo, De'Marrion. My babies. I missed y'all. Look at how grown up y'all are. Come closer so I can get a good look at you."

Walking toward her, I stopped in front of her. She looked up at me as the tears spilled from her eyes.

"De'Maceo, you've grown up to be so handsome. Mama's protector. Always looking out for me and your brother. I'm sorry, baby. I had that monkey on my back, and I swore that I was going to get it off, but it was hard," she spoke to us. As she looked in my eyes, I could see she was being sincere.

"Ma, I gotta question. Be honest with me."

She nodded her head as she wiped the fallen tears. She pulled me into a hug.

"What's my pop's name? And where that nigga at?"

"His name is Demarcius. He doesn't know about you or your brother. I didn't tell him about y'all. That motha-fucka broke my heart. I gave him my everything, and he treated me like a piece of ass. Stay away from him, baby. It's things about him that you don't know. Be careful around him, and don't turn your back on him because he will surely stab you in it." She whispered the last part to me, but I took heed to her warning. Crackheads lied about a lot of shit, but she was giving me a warning. Pulling from her embrace, I stared into her face.

"You serious about getting clean, Ma?"

"Yes, De'Maceo. I know I can never make up for what happened to you or the things I did to you, but I would like to be in my grandchildren's lives. If you don't want me to be, I completely understand," she said.

Before I could respond, Mario chimed in. "Why?" His voice pierced the air.

"Why what, De'Marrion?"

"Why the fuck did you sell me to that fucking pimp? Do you know what that nigga did to me? Do you know I still wake up in cold sweats from that shit? Why would you do me like that? I didn't do a fucking thing to you. I was fucking seven, Ma. Seven! What did I do to deserve for that nigga to touch me?"

"Mario, what are you talking about?"

"You sold me to that fucking pimp, Jason! You know who the fuck I'm talking about."

Her hand shot to her mouth, and she looked at him before approaching him, but he put his hands up, stopping her.

"Mario, he was just supposed to watch you, baby. I had no clue that he had done this to you. Why didn't you tell me? I would never let somebody harm y'all. I don't care how bad of a mother I was. I never harmed y'all, and neither was anybody else going to. Why didn't you tell me?" she cried.

I could tell that she didn't know anything had happened to him.

"I hate you! Straight up! I hate you, and I don't give a fuck what Maceo does about his children, but you can never be around mine. I put that on everything I love. Before you see my kids, they'll see you in a casket. Trust and believe me! Mace, don't trust that bitch."

"De'Marrion, you know I would never hurt you. Have I ever?"

He looked at her with bloodshot eyes. "I hope yo' ass die. And the day that you die, I'ma spit in yo' fucking face. I hate you, bitch."

Mario hated to call a female a bitch, and being that this was our mother, I knew that he was serious. He turned to leave out the door, but she called out to him.

"De'Marrion, I'm sorry!"

"Yeah, you are a sorry bitch! Mace, I'll be in the car."

I nodded my head at him and waited until the door closed. Mario got his answer, but I wanted the rest of mine.

"Where is my pops?"

"I sent him to jail. He didn't know about you boys. He isn't even aware that you're alive. He was in here to visit me a while ago, but I had nothing to say to him. Don't trust him, baby. I've done a lot wrong, but he's a snake, baby. I know all about your dealings in the street, son. Be careful because with him out, he's going to pretend to care, but don't believe it. He seems genuine in the beginning, but slowly, the monster in him surfaces. Watch yo' back, baby. I love you. Go check on your brother," she told me.

I told her I loved her back then left out the room. She gave me a lot to think about and dwell on. I was going to have Chyla get all the info on him. Something about him didn't sit right with me a couple of days ago, and it still didn't. I knew a snake when I saw one, and he was hissing loud as hell.

Taking the elevator back up to ground level, my mind was clouded with all types of thoughts, but mostly my brother. He said he was fine, but the rape was still bothering him. I didn't want to bring it up because he would only lie to me.

Stepping off the elevator, I saw my pops and Mario standing face to face, yelling at each other. Rushing over there, I pushed Mario back and stared down my pops. I don't give a fuck about that nigga like that. It was my brother before anybody.

"Who the fuck are you staring at like that? I don't give a fuck how much taller you are than me. I'm yo' daddy; you not mine."

"I don't give a fuck who yo' pussy ass is. My brother is before any nigga on these streets. I don't give a fuck about what you saying or feeling. I'm my brother's keeper."

He looked at me, licked his bottom lip, then laughed. "A'ight, you got that. But you can't always fight his battles."

"Is that a threat, fuck nigga? Because if it is, I got an extended clip for you and any other bitch-ass nigga that comes for my brother. Speak yo' piece and back the fuck up!" I gritted out.

He looked at me and bobbed his head. "I see y'all li'l niggas get yo' hot-headedness from me, and that's cool and all, but let that be the last time you threaten me. Son or not, I'll knock yo' ass out."

"Pops or not, I'll show up at your funeral in white just to show you how I don't give a fuck. When you speak to my brother, you speaking to me. Believe that! Now, what the fuck is going on?"

"I'll answer that," Chyla said, stepping forward.

"What's up, cuz? What happened?"

Mario made a scoffing noise, and I looked at him. He chilled out for a minute but kept mugging our pops.

"Mario doesn't want to be associated with your father."

"A'ight, I don't see the problem. He's not obligated to get to know no fucking body. If he doesn't want to, he doesn't have to."

"So, fuck me, huh? I didn't even know y'all existed. And I was robbed of even knowing y'all."

"That's a personal problem. I don't care about you or that bitch that gave birth to me. Mace, I'm in the truck, bro." Mario walked off in the direction of the truck.

I looked at my pops, and something about him didn't sit right with me.

"Aye, cuzzo, let me talk to you real quick."

She nodded her head and walked with me. "What's up, Mace?"

"You getting the same vibe from my pops that I'm getting?"

"I'm already on it. When a man's handshake doesn't match his eyes, I already don't trust him. He has a secret security detail following him everywhere."

I bobbed my head, letting what she said sink in.

"I want guards watching my mama around the clock. She knows something about that nigga, and I wanna know what it is. She told me don't trust him, and I believe her. She was too scared and shook when she was talking about him. Mario don't even know I don't trust dude. My mama may have been fucked up, but she would never let anybody harm us. This I know for a fact."

"I got you, Mace. Get home to Saiyah. Just to let you know, I called dibs on being the godmother. The convention is in a week. I expect you at the round table."

I nodded at Delgado and got in my truck. Mario looked at me and shook his head. Starting the car, I pulled back onto the gravel road.

"What's up, bro? What happened back there?" I asked him.

"I don't trust that pussy, and neither should you, bro."

"Oh, trust me, bro. I don't trust that nigga. He ain't allowed around us until I got all facts on him. Something ain't right about him," I told Mario.

"True. But drop me off by Erian's crib. She just told me Saiyah was crying about the pregnancy test. Go talk to her, bro, and be easy on her," he said to me in a sincere voice.

"I got you, bro. Hopefully, it doesn't bring us back to before Macayla. I love that fucking girl too much."

"I know you do, so be easy on her. She's scared. Listen before speaking, bro."

"I hear you, man. I do."

I drove to Erian's apartment, and when I got there, I saw Saiyah getting out of the car. Mario looked over at me and shook his head. I wasn't going to fuck with her. Just wanted to see what was up with my baby.

Parking my truck, I got out and walked up behind her. She didn't even see me. "Say, Miss Lady, can I take you on a date tonight?" I could see her cheeks going up in a smile.

"I don't think I can do that. My man wouldn't appreciate that."

I smiled as I licked my lips. "But yo' man don't got shit to do with me. So, what you say? Dinner and a movie?"

"How about I call my fiancé and see if he wants to come too. Would that be alright?"

"A'ight, now! That's what the fuck I'm talking about. Let that nigga know you got a nigga. But what's up, bae?" I said, pulling her back to me, kissing her neck.

"Nothing, baby. Just coming to check on Erian. But was you serious about the date?"

"Whatever you wanna do. I would rather go home, cook us dinner, nice candlelit romance type shit, take you upstairs to the massage room, and oil your body down before I fuck the shit outta you. So, what you saying, ma? You wanna go out or enjoy our own?"

"Mmmm, I want to enjoy our own. You got a lot of making up to do. Besides, I got a surprise for you. I can give it to you now or later."

The kids had run inside with Mario, so I pulled her back toward my truck and got in the back seat.

"What's this surprise you got for me?"

She reached in her purse and pulled out an envelope. I looked at it suspiciously before opening it up.

"Congrats, Daddy!"

I looked at her to see if this shit was real. I knew that she was pregnant, but not damn near four months. She didn't even look like she was that far along.

"What, man? Hell, nah. You not no four months. Yo, this happened the first time you let me back in my shit. But wait a minute. Are you good? Can you handle this?"

"I'm good, bae. I must see a high-risk doctor, but everything is good so far. Look at him."

I looked at her, and I knew I looked like a Cheshire cat. "Hell, nah! This ain't my boy, though. Quit playing with me," I told her.

Taking the envelope out of my hand, she grabbed the rest of the pictures, and sure enough, it said, *Congrats, Daddy! I'm a boy.*

"Yooo! Yah, you don't even know how a nigga feeling right now. Like, man." I let my head fall back against the seat and let the tears fall. My life was finally coming full circle, and I couldn't believe that I was having another son. I know I should have been this emotional over Li'l Mace, but I wasn't, and it had everything to do with his mother. And even though I didn't regret T'Maceo, he just wasn't in my plans. Saiyah was another story. She was about to bless me with my junior, and I was happy as fuck it was her about to bring him in the world.

"Maceo, stop!" she said to me, pulling me into a hug.

Setting the pictures in the front seat, I pulled her around into my lap. "Thank you, ma. I swear I'm sorry for the fucked-up shit I did with Tee, and I'm sorry for treating you like shit these last couple days. I swear to God that shit won't happen again. I love you, Saiyah, and I want you to know that I proposed because I wanna marry you and be with you for the rest of my life. Hell, yeah, I know it's early and we ain't spent no time together because you went to the rehab, but I'm not in no rush to get married. We can wait two or three years until we ready to do it. I just wanted to let you know that you're where my heart lies. I wanna spend the rest of my life making everything up to you, starting with this pregnancy. I know I wasn't there for Macayla, and that's my fuck up because you kept trying to tell me, and I didn't listen to you. If I could turn back the hands of time, I would listen to you in the drop of a hat. I missed out on time with my baby girl that I can't get back, but most important, I missed out on you," I told her as I kissed her lips.

"I love you, too, Maceo, and I forgive you. I forgave you a long time ago. Do you forgive me?"

"Forgive you for what?"

"For even going to get the abortion without even consulting you. I just didn't know what to do. I was nineteen, about to graduate. I didn't want to hold us back. You had plans, and I didn't want to stop it."

"I forgave you when my baby girl called me Daddy for the first time. I know you don't got no money and don't want to depend on me for nothing, but I owe you that and more. I want all my family under one roof. Will you move in with me, Saiyah? Before you answer, I won't be mad at you for saying no. I just want to wake up with family under one roof. If you need time, I understand."

"Bae, I just want time to live on my own. I've always lived with somebody. I just want time to myself for once. I'll move in right before DJ is born."

"A'ight, I can work with that. In the meantime, let's go check on the kids, and I can plan our night." I kissed her again before getting out and helping her out of the car.

We walked into the apartment and saw the kids sitting with their headphones on, watching their iPads. Shaking my head, I heard Erian and Mario arguing.

"You still blaming me for our son dying. That wasn't my fucking fault, and you know it wasn't. You still fucking childish, and it's a shame that you are because I fucking love yo' stupid ass, but I refuse to keep letting you dangle something that I had no control over, over my fucking head," Mario yelled.

"Fuck you, Mario. You're trying to force me to have a child when I don't want one right now," she snapped.

"If you don't fucking want it, go get the abortion, but just know it's fuck you from here on out. I might love the fuck outta you, but I can surely live without you. You lost one child and want to kill the other. Fuck type of logic is that?"

Looking at Saiyah, I could tell that she knew about their son.

"You knew?" I asked her. "How the fuck did you know something that I don't?"

"Erian got drunk one night and ended up rambling about it. I didn't think anything of the situation. I honestly thought she was drunk, but I guess not."

Knocking on the door, I heard them stop arguing. The door swung open, and Erian looked mad as fuck. Mario was right behind her with a smile on his face.

"What's up, bro? Congrats, sis. At least somebody happy about being pregnant," Mario said.

"She already got one child. Having another one ain't gon' hurt her."

Saiyah looked at Erian, and I could see she took that shit to heart.

"Yo, shut the fuck up. You had the same chance she did. Blame yo'self for stressing over a bitch that I wasn't fucking."

"Fuck you, Mario!" She tried to storm out, but I walked in and pushed her back.

"Yah, get the kids and wait in the car."

She nodded her head and walked away.

"What you want, De'Maceo?" Erian asked.

"One, you can get rid of that attitude. Let me make some shit clear to you. Yo' ass been shading Saiyah for a while now. I didn't peep it at first, but I'm starting to see you got beef with wifey, and I don't like that shit. Saiyah might've said some shit when she was going through her li'l thing, but she ain't never said shit outta pocket about you. You throwing fucking palm trees at her, and I don't appreciate that shit. She loves yo' insecure ass just like my brother do.

"I don't even get in my brother's business, but yo' insecurity is an ugly trait. I happen to know for a fact that my brother ain't never cheated on you, not one fucking time. Not then, and not now, but you standing up here mad about invisible bitches and wanting an abortion. You see how that shit ripped Saiyah and I apart. Can you live without Mario? I knew I couldn't live without Saiyah, but I forced myself to do it. I regret losing all that time with her.

"For Saiyah, I'm dropping bodies and catching cases, but for my brother . . . for my fucking brother, I'm killing the fucking world, and if that includes you, so be it. Mario can be mad at me later about what I said, but I said what I said. Stop being ungrateful. You got one child dead, and you about to kill another. You gon' fuck yo' own head up with that. You're around the same months as Saiyah, if not more. If you get that shit, the first thing you're going to wonder is what yo' child would be like. Would he look like your other child? Who he gon' look like more? That's shit that runs through your head daily because it did for me when I thought yo' girl had an abortion. Be mindful of what you ask for. God has a way of making us regret our decisions or the words leaving our lips."

Turning around, I walked out the room and down the hall. Walking out the door, I locked the bottom lock and headed to my truck. Opening the driver's side door, I slid into the seat.

Saiyah was scrolling through her phone.

"You a'ight, ma?"

She nodded her head, then looked out the window. I was going to say something else but decided to leave well enough alone.

The convention was in a week, and I needed to get prepared. Some of the old heads was about to be sitting at the table. I don't know who was all gon' be there, but this was supposed to be bigger than when the President convenes with his cabinet, and I needed Mario's head in the game. We could use this opportunity to go legit and get out the business once and forever.

The convention had started, and I couldn't believe who Chyla had in there. The Cortez Brothers from North Carolina, Angel, Zell and Kha'Mauri, and most importantly, she had MK, the fucking Midnight Kisser, present. She had all her people that were originally inducted and the newbies, which was us.

"I'm sure y'all are familiar with each other in some sort of way. If not, get familiar with each other. Y'all are here today for two reasons: networking and money. Infamous, Kaine, and Knight, meet Maceo and Mario Reed. You all have a common interest."

We looked at her, confused.

“Dope. Y’all are known to move dope in the fastest and most efficient ways.”

“Zell, meet MK, the one and only Midnight Kisser. She’s just your match. The beast is being tamed right now, and I need you on our job. Kha’Mauri and Angel, you two have the most inventive minds in this room. Your talent with a pen and paper can be transferred to real work. Not just skin. I’m talking buildings, national monuments, etc.”

“Everyone in this room is essential to the Cartel and Mafia. We are one within each other. There is to be no beef, no drama, but there is a snake amongst us. I don’t do snakes, but I will kill those mothafuckas. My reach is long and far, and there happens to be a snake slithering around my fucking feet. I’ve killed for less, and if you don’t want to be a part of our family, stand and leave now.”

Everybody just looked around.

“Alright, we are family, and I expect everyone to act as one. An enemy of mine is an enemy of yours. All traitors will be punished. You’re given a set of rules by which everyone is expected to abide. Any questions, comments, or concerns?” she asked, looking around.

Nobody said nothing, so she proceeded to talk, but I didn’t expect her to be talking to us.

“De’Maceo and De’Marrion, you have a snake slithering at your feet.” She motioned for the doors to open, and in walked Juju, Saiyah’s brother.

“What the fuck? Juju? What the fuck are you doing here?” I asked him.

He just looked at me and shook his head. I knew he had fucked up, but I don’t think he knew how much. Chyla wasn’t one to give second chances. I learned that a long time ago. When I got in this business, niggas who started out with me started dropping like flies. Disrespect and snakes was something she couldn’t tolerate.

"So, you do know him? He told me you would, but I didn't think much of it. But anyways, this fucking punk owes me fifty stacks, and I would like my money. Are you going to pay your brother-in-law's debt, or is he going to give up who he works for?" she taunted.

"I'm not no fucking snitch. You think I give a fuck about death. I welcome that shit with a smile on my face," he said with a smirk on his.

"Juju, who the fuck you working for? I know you loyal, bro, but she not fucking playing with you. Saiyah would die if she knew this shit was going on. Who the fuck is your boss?" I snapped at him.

"Demarcus or Demarcius, some shit like that. He told me to do the shit or he would kill Saiyah. I had to, bro."

I felt my pressure rising.

"I want that bitch-ass nigga head on a platter. What the fuck else do you know, Juju? Don't give me that no-snitching shit. I want an address, a location, something on that nigga, now!" I roared.

"Mace, calm down, bro," Mario said to me.

I looked at that nigga like he lost his mind.

"Calm down? You want me to calm down? Would you be fucking calm if a nigga was trying to kill yo' fucking wife? Fuck calm down. I'm ready to put in work. They don't fucking call me Murder for shit. Fuck this lowkey shit, I'm dropping a body every day until his punk ass shows his face. On my kids, niggas got me fucked up."

"Shit, I'm with that nigga. For my wife, I'm going to war. Aye, bro, if you need my help, I got yo' back. I see wifey means a lot to you," Infamous said.

"Shit, we all got wives in here except my brother, but trust and believe, we down to fuck up another city."

"I appreciate that. If I need y'all, I'll reach it out. Chyla, I'll pay the fifty stacks. Let him go. He was doing it for his sister."

"Fuck that fifty stacks. I got a location on Demarcius now, and he's headed toward your mother," she said.

"Lock down her fucking unit. My mama got something on that nigga, and I wanna know what it is. Shut it down, Chyla."

"He's too close. Your mother is stronger than you give her credit for, Maceo. Let her handle it. The convention is paused as of right now. Maceo and Mario, let's go."

"Aye, no lie, we don't wanna be in y'all business, but shit, we willing to help y'all. This is the part of the convention of networking, and we trying to see how everybody operate."

"Let's go!" Chyla shouted.

Getting up, we all rushed out behind her, got in the elevator, and headed to the basement, which had the detox center connected to it. Rushing through the hall, I got to my mother's room first.

"My! My! How the tables have turned. Why did you do it?" Demarcius taunted my mother.

"Fuck you, Demarcius. You had my son raped by that fucking lowlife. I know you did. You were always so sneaky and manipulative. I would never hurt my boys. I might've been a crackhead and did a lot of shit, but to hurt my boys, our boys, that's a new low for even you."

"Do you think I give a fuck about Mario? I don't like that li'l fucking faggot. You destroyed my life. Had you not set me up, I would've left his punk ass alone. You kept them from me for a reason. I see why Mario, but not Maceo. Maceo, that's my son right there. The blood flowing through his body is ice cold. He has the heart of a lion and the eyes of a monster. That's my boy, not that weak-ass De'Marrion."

I looked at my brother and pulled him to me. "You better not fucking crack. It's affecting you, bro. If I have to lock yo' ass up, I will. You will not give up on me. Don't do it."

He nodded his head. I looked him in his eyes, and they had murder in them.

"Fuck you, Demarcius. Both of my boys are strong, and they will come for you. I'm willing to die for both of my babies. You think I really spent all that money on crack? I took all your fucking money, and my boys will be set. All that crack you sold, all those hoes you pimped, and all those niggas you fucked. Well, yeah, baby, I took all your shit because I deserved it, and so did my babies. I knew you had people looking for me, and that's why I found them safe places to be because I couldn't take care of them. But when I die, they will be richer than you ever know. And thank you for the gift you left me."

"And what fucking gift is that?"

"I'll die soon, courtesy of the AIDS you gave me, you fucking homo. If I could go back in time, I would un-fuck you. Those three minutes weren't worth my life, nor my babies. I'm just glad that both Maceo and Mario didn't get it."

I looked behind me, and I hated that everybody was hearing the cracks in our childhood, but I'm glad I knew the truth.

"Bitch, where is my money?"

I heard a smacking noise and tried to move forward, but I was stopped by the Midnight Kisser. She was a little early, but she put her finger up and told me to wait.

"You'll never find it. You might as well kill me. I have one foot in the grave and the other on top. Mario will never forgive me; I can live with that. Maceo has forgiven me, and I can live with that."

I heard silence. Looking around, I saw MK was gone. *Where the fuck did she go?*

"You know, Midnight strikes once every night, and I'm a little early, but I think you might want to remove your hand from your waist. You're bigger than me, but I wouldn't try whatever plan you're deciding in your head. Y'all can come in."

When we entered the room, MK had her fingers pinched in between his ribs.

"Maceo, Mario, I'm sorry."

Mario looked at our mother, and she shut up.

"You thought we wasn't going to be able to find out about what you did. You have got to be the dumbest nigga I know. You're in my city."

"Li'l nigga, this is my city. Fuck what you're talking about. Somebody get this bitch off me."

MK must've done something to him because the nigga dropped to the ground, unconscious. I looked at her, and she smiled.

"Damn, I still got it! Damn, I love my life. And you, whoever you are," she said, pointing to our mama. "I've killed mothers for fucking less. Don't make me have to kill you. I hate killing mothers, but you seemed to have killed y'all relationship a while ago. Tell your kids the fucking truth about their father. Now!" she gritted out.

"I didn't know about him doing that to you, Mario. I would never hurt y'all. I might have been a bad parent, but I never would put y'all in harm's way. Why would I allow you to get hurt and not Maceo? I love both of y'all. Before y'all were born, I had discovered that y'all father was ripping people off from drugs to cracking cards. He was raking in money. I'm talking by the hundred thousands.

"He had the money, and I was in love with him, so I started helping him. That was, until we started ripping off one of the mobs. I didn't know it at first, but he did. He left me in the dark and left town. I discovered that I was pregnant with you, Maceo, and I was excited to tell him, but before I could, Jorge Torintino kidnapped me and drugged me with heroin. For weeks, he kept me until he realized that I didn't know anything about it. Mace, that's how you were born an addict. It wasn't my fault. After that, he released me with you.

"Your father magically appeared again, but I kept you hidden. I didn't know what to do, but I needed to get all the information from him, just in case something happened to him, so I would have all the money for you,

Mace. But I ended up having sex with him before my six weeks were up, and that's how you were created, Mario.

"Mario, you're my baby boy, and I love you just as much as your brother. I would never hurt you, I swear."

"How did you get AIDS?" Chyla asked her. Her stance let me know she was pissed about the whole situation.

"After I had Mario, I went back to your father because he was gone the entire time of my pregnancy, but the bank account was still building, so I let him. He called while he was having sex, and I was upset when I heard the voice of a man. I knew he was a fucking fag, so I hired someone to follow him. Your father was a fucking male prostitute, fucking high-end rich men. One of them had HIV, but because I didn't know I had it until recently, it turned into AIDS.

"I can't control it anymore, and I'll be dying soon. That's why when Chyla reached out to me, I took the opportunity to get some help."

"Where's the money?" Mario asked her.

"I can't tell y'all because I don't know. All I know is, when you guys bury me, contact Mason and Price law firm. He knows where it's at. His father was an old friend of mine."

"I'ma be one hunnid wit' you, Ma. I'm done with anything that has to do with you. I can't!" Mario left out the room.

Infamous spoke up. "I know what it feels like to have your manhood tested. When I was a li'l shorty, my uncle had his people kidnap me. I don't know if he knew, and maybe he did, but the nigga he had always said some sexual shit to me. I ended up dozing off during the hours that I was kidnapped, and I woke up because I had to pee. At least, I thought I had to, but it was the nigga giving me head. Never, never in my life had I felt so ashamed. I didn't know what it was at first, but after the first time, I fucked a female. I knew that's what I liked, and I also taught a couple bitches how to give me head. I didn't trust niggas or bitches.

"When that fag let me go that day, he made the biggest mistake of his life. I killed that nigga with my bare hands, and from there, I created Supreme. Supreme is my alter ego, and I have no problem bringing him out. Your brother hasn't dealt with his issues. I don't judge a man off what happened to him, but you need to get your brother, man. Go get him."

I looked around, and everybody had these looks on their face.

"Hell, yeah, go get your brother because if it was mine, I would be right there with that nigga. All bosses cry. Go get him, nigga. We got this pussy whenever you want him."

I turned around and ran to my brother. "Mario! Mario! Rio!" I called out to him.

He turned and looked at me. His eyes were bloodshot red. "Bro, like what the fuck? Why the fuck bad shit happens to me? What I do?" Mario said, breaking down.

"Aye! Ain't none of this yo' mothafucking fault. It's my fault. I'm yo' big brother. I'm supposed to protect you."

I heard voices saying, "And if my brother is down, then I am too. If my brother shoots, then I do, too. And if my brother dies, then I die too, because nobody can love my brother like I fucking do. And when they put him in the ground, they better call the morgue because a lot of bloodshed is coming to mothafuckas' doors. If nobody is my brother's keeper, then call me the fucking reaper because I am my brother's mothafucking keeper."

I looked behind him, and the Cortez Brothers were standing behind us, saying it. No lie, I appreciated it.

"Look, man, we know this is a sensitive matter, and we don't get in family business, but we just joined this venture, and we are all brothers in some form or fashion.

I'm the big brother, so I know how it feels to hurt over your brother or feel you couldn't protect them. I'm my brother's keeper all day, and if I couldn't be there, you better believe I'm destroying everything in my path for them. So, the invitation is always open. We family now, so I'm always down to help."

"I appreciate it, bro."

My phone vibrated, and I saw it was from Macayla's phone. I knew something wasn't right.

"Baby girl, what's up?" I asked her. I heard sniffling, and that made me pull away from Mario.

"Macayla! What's wrong, baby girl?"

"Daddy, Mommy is hurt. Bad man hurt her. Hurry!"

The phone slipped from my hand, and I looked at Mario.

"Bro! What's wrong?"

I just looked at him.

"Maceo, what the fuck is going on?"

"Saiyah!"

"What about Saiyah? What the fuck is going on?"

I heard him talking, so I assumed he grabbed my phone.

"Mace, let's go. We gotta get to the hospital, bro. Saiyah was stabbed. Let's go, Mace."

I felt my body moving, but I felt like I was in a dream and needed to wake up.

To Be Continued . . .